YELLOWSTONE BIGFOOT CAMPFIRE STORIES

RUSTY WILSON

For all who love Yellowstone National Park, and for my parents

CONTENTS

FOREWORD

Ever thought about visiting Yellowstone, the world's first national park? Be sure to read these stories before you go, especially if you want to see the hidden side of the park. Or better yet, read them at night by headlamp while camped in one of the park's beautiful campgrounds, listening to wolves howling in the distance—and are you sure it's really wolves?

Fly-fishing guide Rusty Wilson, known as the World's Greatest Bigfoot Story Teller, has spent years collecting these tales from his clients around the campfire, stories guaranteed to make sure you won't want to go out after dark.

Come read about a most unusual occupation in Yellowstone's harsh winters—join an ambitious couple who decide to start a bed and breakfast in the park only to discover they're not particularly wanted—go along on a fant astic vision quest deep in the heart of Yellowstone's highest mountains—come soak in the eerie Boiling River at night—ride along with a snowplow driver for a most unique experience on Yellowstone's wintry roads—witness a Bigfoot tragedy in the making near Old Faithful—experience strange inexplicable events while hiking in the backcountry—help a wildlife biologist with a most unusual and hair-raising task—then read about the strange Yellowstone Fog and the secrets it holds.

But be sure you're not alone in the woods while reading these stories, and whatever you do, don't go hiking by yourself! Another great book from Rusty Wilson, Bigfoot expert and storyteller—tales for both the Bigfoot believer and those who just enjoy a good story.

INTRODUCTION

Greetings, fellow adventurers, to this collection of Bigfoot campfire stories featuring our country's beautiful and amazing Yellowstone National Park, also known as the American Serengeti for its amazing wildlife.

Like most of my stories, these were collected around campfires from my fly-fishing clients, though some were told to me in person. There's nothing like being outdoors around a fire to get folks talking, especially if you add in some mouth-watering dutch-oven cooking.

But a surprising number of stories lately have come from other sources, usually someone telling their friend they should get in touch with me and share their story.

Unlike most Bigfoot research groups, I don't have social media sites where people can post stories, primarily because I don't have time since I'm usually on the river, but also because I don't want people posting hoaxes, which has become more and more common.

How do I know if the stories I put in these collections are true? In all honesty, I don't, just as you can never know if any story is true or not unless you were there. But I do generally only relate stories that come from the person who had the experience, although I do have a few second-hand ones, but only in cases where the original person was unavailable and I feel the person relating the story has a lot of credibility.

It's pretty easy to tell if someone is making things up, for often the stories don't ring true, and sometimes they'll change minor details later without realizing it. This is one reason I like to record the stories, with people's permission, of course, then talk to them again later, usually by phone. And I always change the names and often the places where stories happened, just to give the storyteller anonymity.

Having said that, the stories in this collection all happened where stated. I decided to include the actual locations because I think a dedicated person could figure them out anyway, as Yellowstone National Park has some very distinct regions. In addition, I think people should know what they may possibly encounter when in the park's remote regions, which is where many of these stories took place.

Yellowstone National Park covers over 2.2 million acres, and the Thorofare region has been noted as being the most remote area in the lower 48 states, based on distance from the nearest road as the crow flies, which is around 28 miles there. In addition, Yellowstone has very strict regulations on who can hike where and when, with only a limited number of backcountry permits being issued at any given time.

It therefore only makes sense that an elusive creature like Bigfoot would find the park a great place to live, as long as it could survive the region's brutal winters. Other than Alaska and parts of Canada, Yellowstone probably is one of the few places left where a creature like Bigfoot could walk freely, for the most part.

And walk freely they do, as you'll soon see while reading these stories. I hope you enjoy them, and please don't let the scary ones make you fearful of the park, as it's one of our country's great treasures. Where else can you go hiking in the middle of a 50-mile wide active caldera, seeing all kinds of wildlife in their natural state—maybe even Bigfoot?

So, sit back with a cup of hot chocolate in a big comfy chair or by a campfire and enjoy. And as one story says, hike your own hike, but keep your eyes and ears open for North America's most unique and elusive creature. —Rusty

1

THE WINTERKEEPER

I was in Livingston, Montana one summer's day, having just finished guiding some clients on the Yellowstone River there. Livingston is a big fly-fishing town, as well as an historic railroad town and the original entrance to Yellowstone National Park. I decided to go eat my lunch there at the old station that had once served the first visitors to the park, who came by train.

It was just my luck that one of the big blue Montana Rail Link engines was nearby, waiting to help an incoming grain train across nearby Bozeman Pass. The engineer was standing near the engine, and we got to talking over the whoop sound of the engine's air compressor. His name was Luke, and he told me he used to work in Yellowstone.

Well, one thing led to another, and before I knew it, I'd been invited to dinner at Luke's house, his wife being a fantastic cook. The evening took an unexpected turn when he told me the following story. —Rusty

My name is Luke, and I've been told that when I was a kid I was pretty rambunctious, but let me tell you, 10 years in Yellowstone National Park as a winterkeeper pretty much beat all that out of me.

Winterkeepers are the people who keep the buildings in the park from being crushed by snow—more on that in a minute.

When I worked there, I would work my tail off all winter, then it would take a whole summer of fishing at my parents' place to get enough energy to go do it again the following winter.

What a life—winters in Yellowstone, and summers fishing the Madison River near Ennis, Montana. It doesn't get much better than that.

I was 28 when I quit the winterkeeper job as it got too hard for me, mostly mentally, as the isolation was brutal—and, well, I hate to admit it, but there were things there that I just didn't want to think about anymore. I got my job with Montana Rail Link here in Livingston, working on the railroad.

The railroad's a steady good-paying job, but man, I sure did miss being in Yellowstone at first. I would look south towards the park from the rail yards and wish I was down there, but I guess not bad enough to go back. And I'll get a good retirement from MRL, which I never would have with seasonal work. So, I guess I'm glad I quit winterkeeping.

I was barely 18 when I started in the park, and I got the job only because my dad had worked there for the road department and knew everybody. I'm pretty sure he thought it would help keep me out of trouble, and believe me, it did, cause there's no trouble you can get into out there in the winter.

Well, you *can* get into trouble, but it's the kind of trouble that's likely to kill you, so you have to try and keep your act together. You just don't mess around.

For example, I accidentally locked myself out of my cabin and nearly froze to death my first winter there—it was minus 22 degrees —and when I finally managed to get back in I had minor frostbite on several fingers, in spite of wearing heavy gloves. I rarely locked that door again the whole 10 years I was there, I can tell you.

You can also get into trouble falling when you're shoveling snow off a roof, that kind of thing. The winterkeepers develop a kind of buddy system where you check up on each other, and it's just part of the package of staying alive.

But there's a whole level of trouble out there that I wasn't aware of, and there's only one person I know of who *was* aware of it, and nobody believed him, even though he was a highly respected ranger in the backcountry.

He told me about it when I first started the job, and even though I was inclined to believe him, anytime I'd ask others about it, they would just laugh.

But Ranger Jackson had seen the biggest trouble you can imagine out in the Thorofare, the wildest part of the park, and he wasn't one to play jokes on anyone. He's been retired now for some time, and I never got the chance to tell him about what I saw and that I now truly believe him because I've seen that same trouble myself.

But I can tell you this, I definitely believe Ranger Jackson without a doubt. I don't know if he retired because of what he saw, but I don't think he did. He was a tough guy, legendary actually, for running poachers out of the park, and he wouldn't have let anything run him off.

I myself didn't leave that year I saw it, though I should have, but I did leave two years later when I saw it again. I hardly even had time to pack my stuff that time, I was in such a hurry. And actually, I think that was one of the few times I did lock the door of that cabin.

But before we get into all that, you may ask, what's a winterkeeper?

Winterkeepers in Yellowstone are people who clear the roofs of the buildings there, since annual snowfall can measure from 10 to 20 feet, and the temperatures are often way below zero. This can make the snow consolidate into ice—and bam, there goes your roof, cause it's heavy stuff.

The snow there is dry and fluffy and just falls apart when you try to make a snowball, but once it hardens you can cut it into blocks. I've dealt with ice blocks six or seven feet thick, and this kind of weight can quickly collapse a roof.

A winterkeeper's tools of the trade include a crosscut saw to cut the snow into big blocks and a big flat shovel to push those blocks off the rooftops. Sometimes we'd lay a rope across the length of a roof and then a person at each end on the ground would pull the rope downwards. This would break the contact between the snow and the roof and the snow would come zipping off, but it had to be compacted to do this.

That was my favorite method, because it all came off at once with a very satisfying whump. But either way, you have to climb up on the roof, and that can be a dangerous thing.

You have to be in good shape to be a winterkeeper, but you also have to be pretty tough psychologically to live in Yellowstone through the winter. It's not just the amount of snow and bad weather, but it's also the fact that you're isolated and cut off from civilization. It can get mental real fast, and you'd better be darn self-sufficient. But even with that, it's a beautiful place to live.

Most of Yellowstone shuts down for the winter and all the roads are closed. You can still come in to the Old Faithful Snow Lodge by snowcoach and the Mammoth Hot Springs area by car, but all the other visitor facilities are closed down from mid-October to late April. The only way you can get to other parts of the park is by snowmobile.

And if nobody can get in, you often can't get out, so you have to be able to weather big storms and have lots of supplies. Once in awhile, you can go out on snowmobile to get fresh produce or milk, but it's a long cold journey—a good forty miles, to be exact, from my cabin at Lake Village to the nearest town of West Yellowstone.

So, basically, the winterkeeper's job is to make sure the buildings at Yellowstone don't get destroyed by Old Man Winter. Sometimes we'd also help maintain snowmobile trails and just keep an eye on everything, and I even helped out with a few rescues when snowmobilers got lost. We just did whatever was required, kind of like the early pioneers did to make sure everyone survived.

We had better communications than they did, though, with two-way radios and such. When I first started, there were no cell-phones, but that eventually changed, and some of the people even had satellite TV. They would hole up for the long nights and eat popcorn and watch movies.

But me, I preferred to read and play my guitar. I'm pretty quiet, and that's why I heard things going on that others didn't, for better or for worse.

My cabin was an old 1940s one-room structure with a fireplace and propane heat. It was pretty sturdy, but I had to get up on the roof and clean it off periodically, just like with the other buildings. I haven't been back to the park for a long time, but last time I was there, that old cabin was still standing.

And you know, the scratch marks along the window are still there, though I doubt if anyone but me gives them any mind. If anyone ever notices, they probably think some bear did it.

But nope, it wasn't a bear. If you look closely, you can see they're not claw marks, but more like marks from flat nails, not sharp ones. I still have a photo of that somewhere.

And going back there, even though it was years later, it still gave me the creeps, seeing it again. I now have no desire to go back again, as beautiful as the park is.

My cabin was by Lake Yellowstone, and one of the buildings I helped keep clear was the Lake Hotel. It's a big building and one of the park's most iconic structures. The area called Lake Village has a bunch of cabins we had to clear, and it took several of us to keep it all up to snuff.

I can't remember how many people worked there, as it seemed to vary from year to year, but I do remember a guy named Jimmy who became my best buddy while I was there. Jimmy was from, of all places, Hilo, Hawaii, and his favorite greeting was, "What the heck am I doing here?"

He would sometimes substitute the word *heck* with various cuss words of differing severity, some in what I took to be Hawaiian, and it was a good way to tell what kind of mood he was in that particular day.

He came the same season I did, and none of us expected him to return the following fall, but there he was. I don't know how many seasons he worked there, but he was still at it when I left.

Jimmy soon became known as Heck, and that nickname stuck with him from there afterwards. He lived in a cabin a few down from mine, and we were about the same age, so we naturally ended up hanging around some together in the evenings when we weren't too tired. The cabins between us were uninhabited, being summer cabins.

Sometimes we worked together, sometimes not, depending on what needed doing. But we always checked up on each other in the evening—you'd just bang on the other's door and yell out, "Yo!" and if the person yelled back, you'd know all was OK and go on home.

Well, I'll never forget this night, and I've wondered for years if it didn't have something to do with what happened not too long afterwards. It had been snowing for a week, and we had plenty of work to do. The weather was really getting to us in the cabin fever department.

And yes, we had cabin fever, even though we were outside all day, because of the gray skies and endless melancholic feeling this particular storm brought with it. Some storms break up right away and you get blue skies, but this one just went on and on, each day as dark and depressing as the previous one.

Heck and I both discussed that it might be a good time to head over to West Yellowstone for supplies, even though we were OK, but we nixed the idea based on the whiteout conditions. It would just be too risky. Besides, we needed to stick around and keep the roofs cleared—even one day off would get us behind schedule with all the new snow coming down.

So, we decided instead to have a party. We invited all the other winterkeepers—three or four guys, if I recall—and Heck made a big batch of chili, and I made popcorn in the big pot on top of my woodstove and took it over to his cabin. We decided on having it at his place as it was a little bigger than mine.

Heck always had a big stash of whisky, and he was the kind of guy who liked to share. So, our party got a little wild, which wasn't that unusual.

Winterkeepers basically answer to nobody but themselves, which is why most of them like the job, so they could party as hard as they wanted, their only retribution being the hangover the following day.

To me, popcorn, chili, and whisky sounded like a bad combination, and I declined the spirits, but I will say I enjoyed watching the others get wild and crazy. For a bunch of introverts, they sure let it all hang out.

There'd been lots of wild parties at Heck's, but what made this one stand out was that Heck also had a DVD of the *Boggy Creek Monster*, and everyone watched it while killing off the whiskey, then decided to go outside and whoop it up, literally.

Imagine a bunch of wild men out in the snow, whacking on trees, whooping, screaming, and daring Bigfoot to come visit, and you'll see why I wondered later if this wasn't the catalyst for what was to come. Since it was normally so quiet out there, I'm sure the sound carried for a long ways.

Well, when it was all over, instead of being the designated driver, I was instead the designated "make sure everybody's OK" person. After I was sure everyone was passed out on Heck's floor, I threw some logs in his fireplace, then made my way back to my own cabin through the heavy snowfall, aware that I was getting a bad headache.

Now, I never get headaches, I'm just not made that way. If I get sick, it always starts with tight muscles and aches in my shoulders. And I was in my 20s then and healthy as a mule.

Back at my cabin, I banked the fire, took a couple of aspirin, and crawled into my warm sleeping bag, my rickety but comfy bed feeling pretty good.

As I drifted off, glad I wasn't a drinker, I was kind of puzzled as to why I'd gotten a headache, especially so fast, I mean out of nowhere, and I decided it had to be a contact headache from the whisky fumes. I was so tired that this sounded logical at the time.

The last thing I remembered was hearing the wind blow through the trees, making the branches scratch against the outside of the cabin.

The only problem was, there weren't any trees close to the cabin —but I was sound asleep before that realization caught up with me.

I got up kind of late the next morning, and when I looked out I could see a full-on raging blizzard. I had a strange sense of foreboding, but after a cup of hot coffee and once again banking the fire, I decided I needed to know how my winterkeeper buddies were doing over at Heck's place.

I bundled up and made my way through a good foot of new snow, careful to stay oriented, as it was almost a complete whiteout. Once at Heck's, I banged on the door, and when no one answered, I pushed it open.

The fire was completely out and everyone was still sound asleep on the floor except for Heck, who had miraculously made it to his bed.

I shook my head in disgust, built a new fire, brought in enough wood for the day, started Heck's percolator coffeepot, then went around and tried to rouse everyone.

It wasn't easy, but I finally got everyone up and around, and when I was satisfied that they had their senses back, I went on back to my cabin to make myself some breakfast.

But as I got there, I noticed something really strange—something had walked through the snow behind me as I went to Heck's, actually overstepping my tracks at times. And whatever it was, it sank very deep into the powdery snow, so deep I couldn't make out anything that would tell me if it had hooves or paws. Something had followed me, and it was so heavy it postholed through the snow.

I'll admit it kind of played with my mind, especially since the tracks were so fresh. I looked all around but saw nothing, and it was as if whatever it was had two legs instead of four, and was therefore not a moose, bison, or elk. It sank too deep to be a deer, as they're just not heavy enough like that.

I opened the door and went on inside my cabin, kind of shaken. As I cooked up some eggs and pancakes, I realized that there would be no work today, for the blizzard made it impossible to see anything.

If it hadn't been for the dark shapes of the cabins, I would've been quickly lost just coming back from Heck's.

I decided to stay inside and read a book, or maybe do some of the chores I'd been neglecting, like sewing up my old pair of insulated coveralls. I hoped none of the guys at Heck's would get lost. Maybe they would just stay there and hang out, which would be for the best. Even though we looked out for each other, there was no way I was going to babysit everyone, so I hoped they would just take care of themselves.

When you're in your twenties and working in a situation like we were, you tend to think you're invincible. After all, you can climb like a monkey and cut big blocks of ice and do it all day long. But could these guys make it to their own cabins from Heck's place? I worried about them, even though it wasn't really my deal. But in retrospect, I think I had some kind of intuitive feeling that all was not well.

I spent the morning working on whittling a bird-call whistle, all my chores handily forgotten. I'd been a whittler since I was a kid, my uncle teaching me how, probably hoping, like my dad, that staying busy would keep me out of trouble.

Whittling has a Zen-like quality—your hands are busy and your mind is quiet, and yet it's not completely mindless. As I sat there, it finally occurred to me that I'd heard scratching on the outside of the cabin the night before. And once that thought hit me, I again felt really weird and unsettled, almost like I should flee.

I put my whittling down, bundled up, and went outside to look at the side of the cabin. What I found was totally bizarre—long deep marks that looked almost like they'd been made with a small chisel.

Shaken, I headed for Heck's cabin, even though I knew it was totally insane to be outside in a whiteout. I was very mindful of where I was at every moment, and was very relieved when I got to his door.

When I got there, the fire was again out and not a soul was around. Where had everyone gone? I again started a fire and warmed up for awhile, then decided I should go home, but felt strangely reluctant to go. I felt more like staying there and barring the door.

So staying is exactly what I did, though I didn't bar the door, since the door had no bar. Surely Heck would be back before long, and maybe I could even spend the night at his place. Everyone had extra sleeping bags for exactly that reason, so I knew he could put me up.

I was getting hungry, so I rummaged around Heck's cupboards and found some mac and cheese and started some water boiling on the stove. I knew Heck wouldn't mind, especially since he came over to my place and ate me out of house and home at least once a week.

About the time I got it all made, I could hear the sound of a snowmobile, and sure enough, it stopped by the door. It was Heck, and he looked like those bison over by the geysers when they get snowball beards, those clumps of snow and ice that dangle from their chins.

Heck barely had the machine turned off before he was inside, trailing ice and snow behind him and pulling off his face mask and heavy gloves. He looked surprised to see me.

"I came over to fix you lunch and warm the place up," I lied. "What are you doing out on a day like this?"

"Jeez, bro," he replied. "I was worried sick about you. I stopped by your place and the fire was out and the door wide open. Everything OK?"

I was surprised, as I always make sure my door is closed—maybe not locked, but securely shut.

"Did you go over there just to check on me? Why didn't we run into each other?" I asked.

"I took the guys home," he replied. "It was the only way I could get rid of 'em. I stopped by your place to make sure you were OK, and..."

He hesitated, taking off his heavy boots and coveralls, then continued. "Luke, I went inside and built a fire, and when I went back out, someone had been messing with my machine. It didn't want to start."

Messing with someone's snowmobile in this kind of weather was unheard of—almost an act of premeditated murder.

"Messing with your sled?" I was incredulous. "What makes you think someone did something to it?"

"Luke." Heck looked me square in the eye. "Somebody went into your cabin and messed it up. That's why the door was open. And when I saw that, I got a real strong feeling of dread, like they were still around."

Heck patted his lower back, where I knew he had a concealed gun. We all thought he was crazy to be armed, which was totally illegal in the park, but he worried about wolves and bison and such. None of us worried about the wildlife, so we teased him endlessly about being from Hawaii.

He continued. "When I went outside, I saw tracks, really deep tracks, and I saw that someone had pulled my windshield off. They left snow on the handlebar riser, like they were trying to pull it off, too. I think I surprised them, and who knows what else they might've done."

"What did they do to my cabin?" I asked, worried.

"It looked like they just scattered stuff around. Ate some food. It's not too bad, but maybe you want to go over there and lock it up. And stay there."

"Go out in this weather?" I asked.

Heck rolled his eyes. "I'm going back out and bringing my sled inside. You should do the same. I'll take you over there. The two of us should be enough to scare whoever it is away."

"But why would anyone be out in this storm?" I asked, though I didn't expect an answer to what seemed to be an unanswerable question. I then added, "Your snowmobile won't fit in here. And it had to be a moose."

Heck looked doubtful. "They didn't *break* the windshield, Luke, they popped it off. That takes hands—strong hands. They were intentionally setting me up for failure. You can't see without a windshield in this kind of snow."

I laughed nervously. "You can't see in this weather even with one. And a moose doesn't have intentions, they just live moment to moment. Maybe it was a bison."

"Bison have intentions? And hands?"

"You know what I mean."

"No, Luke, I don't, as per usual."

I decided it would be good to tread lightly, as Heck probably had a hangover. I needed to go back to my cabin, though I dreaded it. I told Heck I would walk back, and left him complaining about having a headache.

The snow was still really coming down, and the lack of definition between the ground and sky made it very difficult to see where I was going. I could still barely make out the other cabins, and was soon back at mine. I didn't waste any time getting there, I can tell you.

I opened the door and went inside, where it appeared that someone had raided my cupboard, tossing everything onto the floor. Most of my food was canned goods, and whoever it was hadn't bothered those, but my boxes of dried goods had been ripped open and partially consumed, the remainder strewn all over the floor, including bread wrappers.

This was puzzling and made me believe the intruder wasn't a person, because nobody can eat six or eight boxes of pancake mix and a half-dozen boxes of cereal, as well as a half-dozen loaves of bread. This was more the work of a bear, but no sane bear would be out and about this time of year, as they were all hibernating.

The cabin had a musky odor that I couldn't identify. I'd smelled lots of bears, as they typically came around the cabins in the fall looking for food. In fact, sometimes they would crawl up against the cabin for warmth at night until they finally decided to hibernate.

But this musky odor was no bear. It was different. It was gaggy and reminded me of an outhouse and a dead animal combined—not to gross you out, I'm just telling it like it was.

I picked up the empty boxes and threw them in the fireplace, swept up the remains of everything on the floor and also threw it in the fire, put the plastic wrappers in my trash box, then proceeded to try to tidy everything back up, ignoring the unsettled feeling that was growing by the minute.

Soon it was time to go outside and get more wood. The fire Heck had built was almost out, as he hadn't set the flue properly, making it burn too hot and fast. I really didn't want to go out in a blizzard, but it was that or eventually freeze.

I was well-versed in the Yellowstone cold and knew not to go outside without being prepared, even if just going out to get wood from next to the cabin, as you never knew what could go wrong.

I dutifully slipped into my insulated coveralls, warm boots, and coat. I grabbed my heavy gloves and opened the door. The woodpile was nearby, and I quickly had a nice pile tossed into the middle of the cabin floor.

The wind was howling, and by the time I was done, several inches of snow had blown inside. As I was sweeping it back out, I thought I could hear something over the wind.

I paused and listened, and it sounded like the combination of someone tearing paper and sneezing. I recognized this as the call of the great gray owl, sometimes called the Ghost of the Forest for its elusiveness, one of the largest owls in the area with a wingspan of five feet. I'd heard its call many times, and it always made me wonder how it made such a strange sound.

I remember thinking it had to be on the roof of the cabin for me to hear it above the wind, which I found odd, as usually birds hunker down in the shelter of trees in storms and don't sit around on roofs practicing their bird calls.

I closed the door and decided to make myself a peanut butter sandwich, but then realized all my bread had been eaten. This was serious, as I didn't want to subsist on canned food alone, though I did have enough I wouldn't starve for awhile. Maybe I could get the guys to all pitch in a loaf or two to help me out.

But I was cabin bound until the storm ended. We were sure going to have a lot of cleaning up to do, and then maybe after that, if the weather held I'd go on out to West Yellowstone and get more fresh food. I could use a break, anyway.

I spent the rest of the day just being bored, wishing the weather would improve, and trying to decide if I shouldn't go on back to Heck's for another visit and bum some bread off him.

But then a thought occurred to me—my cabin had been a source of food for whatever or whoever broke in, and who was to say they wouldn't come back again? Or even try the other cabins?

The thought was kind of nerve wracking, and I decided to stick my head out and see how the storm was coming along, since my window was now iced over.

As I opened the door, the snow that had accumulated against it fell inside, and I had to sweep it back out, the cold air coming in. But it looked like things were improving, as the wind had died down, and instead of nothing but white I could now see a band of dark clouds to the east, telling me the main part of the storm had passed.

I then heard another owl call, and it again sounded like it was on the roof. This one sounded like a saw-whet, one of the smaller owls, with a wing-span of less than two feet. The sound was a series of short toots, like someone playing a one-note recorder.

As a winterkeeper, you can't help but get familiar with the wildlife, and I enjoyed the birds and often fed them nuts and grains when it got really cold, which was against the park's rules, but I did it anyway.

I did this because I felt sorry for them when it was so extreme, but also because I liked having the company. So I'd become somewhat familiar with what was what, even the owls, as I would often hear them in the woods at night.

As I stood listening, I realized that the sound was way too loud for a saw-whet. I mean, in order for the owl to have that kind of volume, it would have to be the size of a goose or even an ostrich.

I suddenly had the strange feeling that the owls on my roof weren't owls at all and that I should get back inside. I closed the door just as half the snow on the roof came down at once, making a loud whump. My doorway was probably now blocked, from the sound of it.

Now what? I was most likely trapped in my own cabin, but at least nothing else could get inside and bother me. Hopefully, Heck and the others would eventually miss me and come over and dig me out.

But so much for going to Heck's and bumming some bread for a sandwich. I knew if worse came to worse, I could crawl out the window, assuming it wasn't frozen shut, but it wasn't something I wanted to do.

And of course since I couldn't have a sandwich, it started sounding better and better until a sandwich became the height of gourmet delicacy and almost worth dying for. I wanted one so bad I felt like moaning—until I realized that something else, something outside actually *was* moaning.

My first thought was that it was Heck or one of the guys messing around, but a repeat performance convinced me it was too loud, and all of a sudden all my denial was gone.

I flashed back on the classic scene in the Boggy Creek Monster where the monster breaks the bathroom window, and I can tell you I was much more scared than that guy had been. I was utterly terrified, for I knew without any doubt that what I was hearing was the same thing.

I recalled talking to Ranger Jackson about what he'd seen up on the Thorofare, and I knew that what had been theoretical to me then was now reality. I knew I was hearing a Bigfoot, complete with their owl imitations, which seemed to be one of their preferred means of communication. And since they were communicating, there had to be more than one. This was the kind of trouble Jackson had talked about, except he'd only seen one.

Now it all made sense—the deep tracks, something pulling off Heck's snowmobile windshield, the raiding of my cabin, the owl sounds, all of it. And it all started with the guys being idiots and whooping and hollering after watching that dumb movie. I could see the Boggy Creek monster clearly in my mind's eye, and I knew it had to be just like the one on my roof.

Now, from nowhere, I started getting another headache. Everything started feeling fuzzy and disoriented. I grabbed my water jug and drank a bunch, thinking maybe I was dehydrated, but the headache just got worse.

I now started to feel panicked. I needed to get over to Heck's place. I couldn't deal with this by myself. I needed his help. But the snowslide off my roof had trapped me—or had it? I realized I hadn't actually tried to open the door and verify that.

Since the door opened inwards, I was able to slowly pull it open a crack and look out. The snow was about three feet deep, and I was sure I could dig my way out.

I listened for awhile, but heard nothing, no more owls. The sky was turning a pale pink and I could see stars trying to break through the thinning cloud cover. If I wanted to get going, I needed to make a break for it now, not later.

I kept a shovel inside for this very purpose, and after I'd bundled up, it didn't take long to dig a path through the snow, even though it was wetter and heavier than normal. I was wary, looking all around and up and down while doing this, totally panicked and scared to death.

And even though I hadn't seen the Bigfoot, I could picture it in my mind as if I had, only maybe even bigger and uglier than I imagined. It became the ugliest most menacing thing imaginable with each shovel of snow. As you've probably guessed by now, I have a good imagination, but I really preferred to be imagining things like gourmet sandwiches.

Going back inside, I stoked the fire, then stuck some candy bars in my coat pockets along with a water bottle, slipping my headlamp onto my forehead. I would hopefully not need it, but if I got disoriented, it could be a lifesaver.

All the time I was doing all this, the rational part of my mind was saying to stay put, stay home, don't go out. First, if there really are Bigfoot around, you'll be more vulnerable, and second, with the skies clearing, it was going to be bitter cold. Not a good night to be out.

I suddenly wished I had a gun like Heck's, and this was part of my rationale for going to his place. His place seemed safer, for we could defend ourselves, and there was safety in numbers.

I stepped outside and pulled the door tightly shut, again looking around. It was now dusk, but I figured I could make it to Heck's place pretty quickly and beat the dark.

Keep in mind that along with my anxiety and fear was what had become a pulsing headache, and it was getting harder and harder to think straight. But I knew the way well and was soon making a beeline for his cabin.

I'm not sure what happened after that, but I vaguely remember something following me, making short whooping sounds with a kind of raspy voice. I doubled back into the trees, trying to ditch it. It didn't seem particularly menacing, more like it was following me for its own entertainment, so I finally came back out and started wandering through the forest, amazed at how beautiful it was with all the new snow, totally forgetting where I was going.

The next thing I knew, I was on the back of Heck's snowmobile and he was berating me for being an idiot and saying that if it hadn't been for my headlamp, he would've never seen me. He took me back to his cabin, where we tried to sort out what had happened.

Apparently he went to my place to check on me and found my tracks. The sun was setting, and the tracks were going the opposite direction of his cabin. He wasn't sure whether to go get the others to help search for me or to set out himself, hoping that I wasn't far off and he could quickly find me.

He decided to follow my tracks, but it was soon so dark he could barely make them out, even with his headlight on, and he was getting worried about getting lost himself.

He was about ready to turn around and go get help when he heard a crashing through the woods. He was pretty sure he'd stirred up some bison and was turning around when he saw a light where the sound came from.

He drove to the light, where he found me wandering around, then quickly got me on the back of the sled and headed back, hell bent. He said he could hear something big following us through the woods, breaking branches as if it was really angry.

Finally back at his cabin, he helped me inside and then locked the door, putting his loaded gun in a handy spot. I was freezing, so he made me some hot tea and pulled my chair up next to the fire.

He told me that I was totally disoriented and thought we were in an airplane concourse getting ready to fly to Hawaii. I also kept telling him we were going to get in a lot of trouble for abandoning our jobs and letting the snow crash in all the roofs.

I don't remember any of this, but I guess I believe him when he says it happened. The only thing I do remember is wandering through the woods, looking at the starlight shadows of the trees.

I do recall being vaguely irritated when a voice told me to turn on my headlamp. I tried arguing that it would wipe out the shadows, but the voice got angry, telling me to turn it on.

If you're not familiar with starlight shadows, in Yellowstone the winter snow is so smooth and the skies so dark that it's possible to see shadows created by the starlight. The shadows are faint, and it takes your eyes awhile to get acclimated to the dark, but they're actually really magical.

I asked Heck if he'd told me to turn on my light, and he looked puzzled. "Why would I tell you to turn on your light if I'd already found you?" I agreed it made no sense, but I distinctly remember someone telling me to do just that.

When Heck asked me what the voice sounded like, I told him it was muddled. He shook his head and asked, "How can a voice be like that?" I said I didn't know, and he dropped it.

We hunkered down by the fire and were real quiet, both of us spooked and afraid to talk. My headache was totally gone, and I told Heck about hearing the owls and feeling claustrophobic and feeling like I had to get out of the cabin no matter what.

He didn't say much, but then told me he thought I'd been the victim of some kind of mind control, so we talked some more about that, and I asked him why a Bigfoot, if that's what it was, would mess with my mind and then help me get rescued. It didn't make sense. But then, to most people, the idea of Bigfoot even existing doesn't make sense. But Heck said maybe it was curious but didn't want me to die, so it had told me to turn on my light so he would see me.

After sitting silent a bit longer, Heck finally got up and picked up the Boggy Creek Monster DVD, opened the cabin door, and threw it out into the snow as far as he could.

The rest of the night was uneventful, and I went back to my cabin the next day, ate breakfast, and we all went back to work cleaning roofs.

I left a month or so after all this happened, when the job ended for the season. I went back for two more years, always kind of hesitant to return, but when they promised me I could move over to the Old Faithful Inn area, I felt like it would be OK.

I worked two winters there, and one morning, as I was climbing off a roof, job done, I heard that same saw-whet owl hooting at me.

For a minute I thought it really was an owl, but when a strange feeling came over me and I started getting a headache, I went to my supervisor immediately and told him I had to leave.

I was out of there within three hours, all my stuff packed and on a snowcoach. I locked the door to my cabin and didn't go back to the park for many years, and I never forgot the sound of that mudded voice telling me to turn on my headlamp.

Livingston's only about an hour from the park, so it's very possible that Bigfoot wanders up here once in awhile. But we live right in the middle of town, and when I'm on that train engine, I don't worry about anything.

But I can tell you this, even though I did at first, I now never feel any desire to go back down into Yellowstone National Park. And when summer comes and the town fills with tourists, I look at them and think, "You guys have no idea what's down there or you'd just stay here and have a beer or two."

2

THE INHOLDING

I'm not out in Oregon very often—in fact, I haven't been there for a number of years, so when a friend told me they had a cousin there named Marty that I should talk to, I wasn't sure how it would come about, if ever.

But it wasn't long afterwards that I got a call from Marty saying he and his wife Gabby were coming to Colorado to look into buying a small vineyard, and would I like to come meet them?

My wife Sarah loves the little town of Palisade, home of Colorado's wine district, so we took our camping gear and spent the weekend camped nearby, inviting Marty and Gabby to meet us over a campfire. We all really hit it off and had a great time, and they had quite a story. —Rusty

My name is Marty, and I can still remember the ad, almost verbatim, that started everything: *Yellowstone Park from your deck! If you love the area and want to be in America's first national park, this is the property for you, as well as your family, with five bedrooms and six baths.*

Well, who wouldn't want to see a national park from their deck? Most of us have to work, and we have to live wherever our work is, so we get to see national parks only on our vacations.

My wife Gabby and I weren't even in the market for a house, but for some reason, the ad stuck with me, and I couldn't get it out of my mind. With that many bedrooms and baths, it was way too big for us, as our two kids had flown the coop years before.

The land is a mining inholding from the 1800s, a privately owned piece predating the designation of the park. This makes it truly one of a kind, as you will actually be surrounded by Yellowstone.

Well-cared for, the home sits on ten acres with one-half acre fenced, and features wood floors, vaulted ceilings in the living area, updated bathrooms and kitchen, as well as a hot tub and expansive decks. Deer and bighorn sheep may visit, as well as bison, elk, and even an occasional wolf. The house will be sold furnished with the exception of a few items of personal or sentimental value to the seller. The sellers are motivated and will entertain all offers.

Gabby and I had our own house in Oregon, along with more furnishings than we knew what to do with, having lived in that same house for most of our married lives. If we were somehow to miraculously decide to move, we needed a house that was empty, not one full of someone else's furniture.

I don't know, maybe I was bored. Ironically, I wasn't the one that usually would look at house ads, that was more Gabby's hobby. I always told her she should've been a real-estate agent, because she seemed to enjoy looking at glossy magazines of fancy houses.

She always said that she would love to run a bed-and-breakfast, until I would remind her of how much work it was. We'd stayed at a few, which were nice, but it seemed to me that running one wouldn't be much more than being a glorified cook and housekeeper. And based on the numbers of ones she would find for sale, it seemed like a burnout profession.

But that ad stayed with me. Maybe I was feeling a little bit guilty. I knew Gabby would be perfect for running a bed-and-breakfast, but I really wasn't interested in all that daily grunt work myself.

We had discussed it a lot, and she said we could always hire out some of the work, but I knew myself better than that. I wouldn't be able to bear paying someone for work I could do myself.

We were both retired, but still energetic and in good shape. Gabby had been a nurse, so she was good at taking care of people, and she loved to garden and cook, all attributes that would serve a B&B proprietor well.

I spent my whole career in high-school administration, and to be honest, I was pretty burned out with people in general. My job had been basically one of babysitting both kids and adults, putting out fires, and trying to make everything hang together.

And some of the biggest fires I'd had to put out involved not the students, but their parents, so I knew what dealing with adults was all about. Personally, I preferred the students. Sure, I'd been paid well, but I had just gotten used to the peace and quiet of being retired, and I sure didn't want to give that up.

I recall once telling Gabby that I'd be happy to do a B&B with her if we only allowed high-school kids or younger. She thought I was just being funny.

So, back to that ad for the house. The town was one of those close to the park, and I'd rather not say which one, since the woman who sold us the house still lives there, as far as I know, though I don't think she's an agent anymore. You can narrow it down to one of four —Cooke City, Cody, West Yellowstone, or Gardiner—but that's it.

About the only thing we did right through all of this was to keep our house in Oregon. Part of the reason we kept it initially was because we didn't want to get rid of all of our stuff.

OK, so back to the ad, which I for some reason couldn't get out of my mind. The one thing I think that made the difference was this part:

Detached heated garage includes a small private apartment. The garage has extensive shelves and space for a hobby or two and comes with numerous power tools.

I'd always wanted to get into woodworking, something my dad did as a hobby. He'd actually taught me quite a bit, and his specialty was making guitars. I still have two of them, and they're beautiful, with inlaid ivory and ebony.

I could see myself holed up in that garage making cool stuff while

Gabby entertained people, and I could even stay in the apartment when the guests got too overpowering. I could set up my own little world out there while Gabby socialized. I would then help her after everyone was gone.

Gabby and I had been to Yellowstone two years earlier, staying in this same little town and enjoying ourselves immensely. She'd even remarked that she would like to live there someday.

I had to admit it was a beautiful place, but I also wondered what the town was like in the winter, for Yellowstone is well-known for getting lots of snow.

I was happy in Oregon, for we lived in a small town in the Willamette Valley, famous for growing lavender, iris, dahlias, and tulips, as well as for its wineries. It had a mild climate, and there was lots to do. Plus, having lived there our entire lives, we had tons of friends and family there.

So why couldn't I get this ad out of my mind? The place seemed priced well enough, and we could probably swing the loan, although I wasn't sure if I wanted to be in debt again, our house being paid off.

But if we didn't like it, surely we could sell it, especially if it had a B&B business included. Maybe we should do it for a few years, then sell it and make a little money while having lived in Yellowstone.

The exterior is a private oasis with a beautifully landscaped and treed lawn. So sit back, relax and experience those Yellowstone views as they were meant to be. This one is special.

Well, they were all special, weren't they? But without even really thinking about it, I dialed the agent.

Her name was Sue, and the first thing she mentioned was that the price had just been reduced a bunch and the owners really needed to sell, as they were having financial difficulties. When could we come see it?

Telling potential buyers that your clients are in financial trouble isn't considered the most ethical thing to do, but Sue explained that she had their permission to say this, as they wanted people to know they were super eager to sell and would work with whatever was offered.

Well, a few red flags went up, but not enough, I guess, because I was soon downloading a video tour of the house that Sue sent.

The new price should've also set off a few red flags, but instead, I guess it brought out my greed—you know, that thing of getting a steal of a deal, even if it's something you really weren't even sure you wanted? You buy it because it's such a good deal you have to or you'll never forgive yourself for losing out? Yeah, right, and at my age, I really should've known better.

I pride myself for using reason, but this time, my emotions got the better of me. Plus, I wanted to make Gabby happy—or so I said. Good excuse, but pretty much true. And boy, did it end up having the opposite effect, but more on that later.

The house was beautiful, the decor very tasteful, the furniture really nice, and the views were incredible, with forest all around and big mountains in the distance.

How did they get such good views? Well, when the video showed the road in, I understood—the views were good because you were basically on the top of a mountain looking across a huge valley at other big mountains, with town a good 10 miles away.

No wonder you had wolves in your front yard, I thought. And this definitely looked like a summer-only place.

But as if she knew what I'd be thinking, Sue had added a note that said it was easily accessible in the winter if you kept it plowed and had a four-wheel drive.

Well shoot, I thought, about anyplace was accessible under those conditions. Oh, and the place came with a pickup that had a plow attached. Handy. I was beginning to see why it hadn't sold and why they'd dropped the price. Who wanted to spend all winter plowing and fighting to get in and out?

If I'd had any brains, I would've dropped the whole idea right then and there, but instead, I was even more intrigued. What would it be like to live in a place like that, where you were basically surrounded by wilderness, and Yellowstone wilderness at that?

Yellowstone was special partly because of all the many and

diverse species of wildlife there. It was an almost intact ecosystem, having been named the world's first national park in 1872.

So, instead of letting it go, I told Gabby, and within a week we were flying from Portland to the nearest airport, where we rented an all-wheel-drive Subaru and headed to the house in Yellowstone.

It was late spring, and even though the road had been recently plowed and we didn't have any trouble getting in, there were two-foot drifts all around the house. We stood on the deck as Sue pointed out the property lines, as we weren't even able to walk around. The place obviously got a lot of snow.

Gabby and I had already decided we would go back to Oregon for the winters, giving us the best of both worlds. We would just winterize the place, then come back when the snows melted.

But when I asked Sue about how safe the house would be with no one around, another red flag went up. She laughed nervously and remarked that the owners had installed an alarm system.

The entire house ran on solar, and a de-icing system had been installed on the roof to keep snow from getting too deep, and there were security cameras all around. I once again wondered why you'd need security cameras up there in the winter, but Sue then started telling Gabby about the wine cellar, and I got the distinct feeling she didn't want to continue down that line of discussion.

When I asked who had plowed the drive so we could get in, Sue said there'd been a fellow staying in the apartment through the winter, but he'd just left. He used a snowmobile in the winter, but if anyone were coming, he would plow the road.

I asked Sue if he might be willing to continue staying there in the winters, but she said he'd burned out and was going back to Nebraska. This, I found out later, was another red flag.

We walked all through the house, checking everything out, and I finally went out to the garage, leaving Sue and Gabby talking.

The garage was really nice with a concrete floor stained a deep red, lots of well-built shelves, and more tools than I could ever use. It also had a huge upright freezer.

When I opened the door to the small apartment, I was pleasantly surprised by nice big windows that looked down a small glade lined by huge pines. The views here were every bit as nice as those from the house, if not better.

You could tell that someone had lived there and hadn't cleaned it all that well when they left, but a little elbow grease and paint would bring it back.

I opened the fridge to see if it was on and was surprised to find it was pretty well-stocked with food, most of which looked fresh. The guy who'd been living there apparently had forgotten to clean it out when he left. I'd tell Sue and she could take it all home with her.

I was actually kind of enjoying my time away from Gabby and Sue, whose enthusiasm was starting to wear me down, so I hung out there for awhile, sitting on the western-decor couch and picking up a notebook from off the coffee table.

Inside was a sort of journal, which surprised me, another thing the previous tenant had apparently left behind. He must've left in a hurry, I mused, reading a couple of his entries, curious, but not wanting to pry. I could also give this to Sue to somehow get back to him.

Ap. 6. Big snow, howled all nite. Out of venison. Leave me alone, dammit. Want to go, but whiteout.

Ap. 8. Up all nite. Howling. Sketchy. Try to get out tom.

Ap. 9. Damn snowmachine won't start. Worked on it all day.

Ap. 10. Will leave today if I have to walk out. Hate this place. Some poor fools are coming to look at it. Hope it rots since they all lied to me. I'll be gone. Wish I could tell the new people.

I stuck the notebook in my pocket, alarmed. The fellow had left the day before we arrived. Maybe Sue would have his number so I could talk to him. I found his entries disconcerting.

I made my way back to the house, determined not to buy the place. I would show the notebook to Gabby, and I was sure she'd feel the same way.

Once back down off the mountain, Gabby and I went to our motel room to discuss everything, but we soon had a call from Sue inviting us to dinner at a nice restaurant. She said she'd just talked to the owners and had an offer for us.

I was puzzled. Wasn't it usually the other way around, with the buyers making an offer?

We actually preferred to stay in and talk about things but felt we couldn't refuse, so we met Sue for dinner. Well, come to find out, the owners had just dropped another fifteen-grand off the price and it was now at about half of their starting price. The fact that they were so eager to sell was again a red flag. Had something bad happened there?

At this point, I was ready to can the whole deal, but back at the motel, Gabby outlined how she was going to market the property and make enough money to pay it off in a few years. She'd already run the numbers, and if she could keep it almost full for six years from May through October, it would pay itself off.

I found her nightly pricing to be exorbitant, but she said having an inholding in Yellowstone National Park was priceless. If so, why was it being sold so cheap? I asked, but she ignored me.

She'd even written up a description of the place, calling it the *Bear's Den*:

Come see Yellowstone as few get to see it, from a private mountain retreat inside the park! Your dream vacation will include gourmet break-fasts on expansive decks, afternoons hiking our private trails or reading a book, and fabulous dinners while watching the sunset, followed by an evening campfire with smores. You'll see deer and elk and black bear from your bedroom windows, and maybe even a bison, grizzly, or wolf! (The property is fenced, so you'll be perfectly safe.) Photographers are welcome. We are located on a mountain top actually within Yellowstone National Park and will pick you up in town or you can drive yourself here, though an all-wheel drive vehicle is necessary. Come enjoy the wilds in an unforget-table luxurious setting!

She was excited, and I felt a sinking feeling, like it was a done deal. Sue had said the place was zoned for multi-use, so we could do whatever we wanted with it, and a B&B would be welcomed by the tourism board there.

She had already made up a list of property inspectors and title companies we could pick from. A well inspection had been recently done. This should've been another red flag, for someone had apparently liked the place well enough to have a well inspection done, then had passed on it.

Sue and Gabby were both ready to sign the papers, right then and there. I felt a strange reluctance, not at all like the excitement one should feel when buying such a place. In fact, the closer it got to being a done deal, the more dread I felt.

After we were back in our room, I told Gabby what I was feeling. The look on her face said she was very disappointed, but she said we needed to do what was right and best for both of us. We decided to sleep on it. I decided I'd show her the notebook in the morning, as I was too tired to want to discuss it.

I woke in the middle of the night to a cold sweat. I'd been dreaming about something frightening, but I couldn't remember what it was. I didn't want to wake Gabby, so I got up and quietly paced back and forth in the room. I hadn't felt this unsettled for many years, if ever. My gut was trying to tell me something.

I asked Gabby the next morning if she'd felt anything unusual about the house, but she said no. This made me feel better, because she was usually the one more sensitive to her surroundings. If the place felt OK to her, then I was probably just being super paranoid or something.

When I showed her the notebook, she thoughtfully said, "Marty, I think the winter just got to him. Being alone up there would make me go nuts, too." I could tell her mind was made up.

So, the next day we signed a contract down at Sue's office, offering them a good deal less than they were now asking. I'm not much of a bargainer and this was Gabby's idea, but with a quick phone call to the owners by Sue, the offer was accepted.

The contract was still contingent on an inspection, but we didn't expect anything unusual there. And two weeks later, we paid cash for a property on a mountaintop actually inside Yellowstone National Park.

Friends later asked if we thought Sue knew anything about what was going on up there, and I have to say I think she did. When I asked her for the caretaker's number, she didn't have it. Later, she seemed to disappear and was impossible to contact, though I knew she still lived there.

Gabby and I were soon back in Oregon, packing our personal things and getting ready to spend the summer in the new house. She was already working with a designer to make a logo and advertising materials, and she'd already put ads all over the internet. And we hadn't been home more than a week when she already had the place almost completely booked, starting in three weeks.

This surprised her as much as me, and so, in order to get ready, she and our daughter, Lizzie, headed out to the new house, pulling a small trailer with things she wanted for the B&B and a few personal items. Lizzie was a middle school P.E. teacher and had the summer off, so she would go help Gabby run the place.

I would stay in Oregon and get our house ready for our absence, setting up the automatic sprinkler systems and battening down the hatches. I would also take care of our two collies, Biscuit and Wheatie, until Gabby gave the word for us to come join them.

I was glad to not be going this time, though I didn't mention that to Gabby. In fact, I was dreading going, and, knowing it was my idea in the first place, I kicked myself over it.

Weeks passed, and I talked daily with Gabby, who gave me progress reports. At least the cell service there was good, being up on a mountain. She and Lizzie were having a great time, entertaining people and coming up with new recipes and things to cook.

Reviews on the webpage for the B&B were starting to come in, and it sounded like things were going really well:

This side of heaven, and great hospitality. The stars are unbelievably bright and the air is crisp. Gabby is a great cook! Enjoyed the serenity! Kathy and Bill

Gabby and Lizzie are the most caring hosts we've ever had. Really made sure we had the best Yellowstone trip possible, cooked us a great breakfast and dinner each day, and made us feel more than at home. Highly recom-

mend this place to anyone wanting to see one of the most beautiful places on earth. Jack and Mary

In spite of all the glowing reports, I still had no desire to go there, even though I missed my wife. She and Lizzie had now been there several weeks, and I still didn't know when I would join them. Gabby was beginning to get frustrated with me, wanting me to come out.

But it wasn't long before the reviews started to take a turn:

Friendly hosts will greet you with warm fresh-baked cookies at this beautiful place. Be sure to not underestimate the time it will take to drive there, and I highly recommend making the drive before sunset. Going after dark gets a little creepy. Enough said, just go before dusk. In all other ways it's well worth every penny. Gina

Lizzie and Gabby make a delicious breakfast and dinner, and the place is super comfortable. This is a phenomenal experience for those looking for an authentic experience near Yellowstone. But do stay inside the fence at night. We thought we saw a grizzly outside one evening, and it was pretty scary, but just part of being in the wilderness. Ben and Julie

But one day, two reviews were posted that had me making plans to get out there ASAP, as I worried if Gabby and Lizzie might be in danger.

Instead of the Bear's Den, this place should be called the Bear Trap, because you feel like you're trapped and somebody's bait. We heard weird howling all night, and when talking about it with the other guests, we all decided there was no way it could be wolves, even though the manager said it was. We'll never come back and anyone who goes up there should be very very careful about going outside, especially at night. After that, I wouldn't even sit on the deck in the daytime. We left early. J. and G.

All I can say is that it's a slice of heaven and the hosts are wonderful, but there's something out there. I won't venture to guess what it is, but it sounds angry. We were terrified by weird noises all night. Yellowstone's a wild place, and something didn't want us there. Couldn't wait to leave. Lois

After reading the new reviews, I tried calling Gabby, but there was no answer. I then tried Lizzie's number with the same result.

Well, this was disconcerting. Where was everybody? I called my son, Kevin, and asked if he would mind dogsitting for a week or two, then I arranged a flight and packed my bags.

I dropped the dogs off on the way to the airport, trying not to sound too concerned while talking to Kevin. But he also became worried and made me promise to stay in touch and let him know what was going on.

I'd hoped someone would pick me up at the airport, but I still hadn't been able to get anyone on the phone, so I rented an SUV, wanting to be sure I could get up the road to the house.

But while driving up the road, I wasn't prepared for what I found. A very large tree had fallen across the road, blocking traffic, with no way to go around.

I got out and surveyed the situation, and at first it looked like the tree had fallen naturally, as the log had big splinters instead of cut marks. It was odd, though, because it wasn't rotted or anything, and there was no reason for it to fall. None of the other trees looked like there'd been a big wind or anything, it was just this one tree.

Nevertheless, I was stuck and couldn't get to the house. It was too far to hike in, so I had no choice but to turn around and go back to town.

There, I finally located a guy who could go up and remove the log, and a couple of hours later, the road was cleared. The guy, Gus, was a timberman and cut the log into several pieces with a chainsaw and then pulled them to the side with his winch.

When I paid him, I asked if he had any idea what had caused the log to fall in the first place, and his answer kind of gave me the creeps.

"This is the fourth or fifth log I've cleared off this road," he answered. "None of them seemed to have any reason to fall—it's almost as if somebody knocked them over, except they're all too big."

He shook his head, then continued. "You couldn't pay me enough to live up here. You guys are probably at least the third or fourth owners of this place in as many years. Nobody stays very long. There's been rumors around this mountain since I was a kid growing up here."

I felt kind of sick, knowing I should've listened to my intuition and not gone along with Gabby.

"What kind of rumors?" I asked.

"You guys own this place, right? If I were you, I'd get out, not tomorrow, but today. My grandfather built this road years ago. He went to a lot of trouble and work to get up onto the mountain where he had the rights to some really nice big old-growth trees. This was years ago, mind you, and he never got one tree off this mountain. Every time he would turn around, a piece of equipment would be destroyed, and he couldn't keep workers. He finally gave up and abandoned it."

"Why?" I asked. "What was going on?"

"This mountain is right in the middle of the reserve, and there's things in there that nobody knows about, things that have been there since forever ago. These things don't want anybody around bothering their habitat. I can't say I blame them, actually. Did your realtor tell you why the previous people left?"

"No."

"Was it Sue Fletcher? She's made a pretty good living selling this house over and over, and that's about all I'm going to say about that. I do know for a fact that at least two people have gone missing on this mountain. Both were hikers, missing at different times, and neither has ever been found."

I was dumbstruck at this information.

"My daughter and wife are up there at the house," I said in a panic. "I haven't been able to get ahold of either of them since day before yesterday. I'm worried sick."

"Oh, they're the ones who started a B&B up there, eh? My wife works at the sheriff's office, she's a dispatcher, and she told me recently several reports came in from people staying up there."

I felt even more panicked. "Reports? What kind of reports?"

Gus replied, "Like I said, there's creatures there who call it home. They're mad. People have reported strange howlings and growls and all kinds of threatening sounds like that, and one guy said something chased him down the road here as he drove out."

I suddenly felt a sense of doom. I asked, "Gus, would you mind driving up there with me? I sure could use some moral support, and if something is wrong, I'm going to need help."

Gus was silent, shuffling back and forth on his feet, then finally replied, "You know, the last thing I want to do is go up this mountain, especially after seeing this downed tree. Something doesn't want anybody up there, but if your wife and daughter are still up there, we need to do something. I need to call my wife first and let her know what's going on, though."

I was soon following Gus's truck, half expecting to come across another downed tree, his chainsaw and equipment rattling around in the bed of his pickup with every bump.

We were soon at the house, where I could see Gabby's car parked right where it should be. It didn't appear that there were any guests, and everything looked fine.

We went inside, but no one was around. After carefully searching the entire house, we found nobody. Gabby and Lizzie were both gone, but there were no signs of anything amiss.

"Could they be out hiking or something?" Gus asked.

"I don't think so," I replied. "Like I said, I haven't been able to get ahold of anyone for awhile. I really think something's wrong, Gus. It's not like Gabby, she calls me every single day."

Gus shrugged his shoulders. "You want me to call the sheriff?"

"There's one last place we need to look," I replied. "There's a little apartment attached to the garage."

We searched the garage and the apartment, but found nobody. I then sat down on a chair, holding my head in my hands, feeling like crying.

It was then that I heard something, a muffled sound, a banging, coming from somewhere nearby. Gus held up his hand as if to say be quiet.

We followed the sound to the large upright freezer in the corner of the garage. The shelves had been tossed onto the floor, and someone was inside, pounding.

Gus opened the door, and out came Gabby. She looked like death warmed over, and I grabbed her before she could fall to the floor, helping her into a chair.

"What in the heck were you doing in there?" I asked. "You okay?"

"Where's Lizzie?" she asked.

"I was hoping you could answer that question," I replied. "But why were you in the freezer?"

"It's turned off," Gabby said. "I was hiding, but then I couldn't get the door open."

"You're lucky you didn't smother to death," said Gus. "How long were you in there?"

"I don't know. A few hours. I could breathe—the drain plug's open, plus the seal is shot," Gabby replied. "I almost had it open when I heard you guys. But we have to find Lizzie." Gabby was now getting panicked.

"Gabby," I said soothingly, putting my arm around her shoulders. "What were you hiding from?"

"Marty, we have to find Lizzie and get out of here. Last I saw her, she was running into the forest, trying to divert the thing from following me. Nobody will believe me." She now started sobbing.

Gus now took her by the hand and said, "Gabby, I'm Gus, and I know exactly what you saw. I believe you. Those things have been here for years."

"I've been trying to call you guys for two days," I added.

Gabby looked surprised, then said, "There was weird stuff going on night before last and everyone left. Lizzie wanted to go to town, but I was too afraid to go in the dark. Everyone's been leaving early, because this thing keeps coming around. Its screams and howls are terrifying."

"After everyone left, it came into the yard, and Lizzie and I hid in the pump house. We were there all night. I never want to go through that again."

I could tell it was all she could do to not start crying again. She continued. "The next morning, we thought it was gone, and we went back into the house to get our stuff so we could leave, but it came back. Lizzie screamed at me to go hide. I didn't know what to do. I wanted to help her, but she kept yelling at me to go hide, and I knew there was nothing I could do, so I hid. She took off running and it followed her. We have to find Lizzie."

Gabby was talking so fast I could barely keep up with her, and I knew she was on the verge of complete collapse.

Now Gus was on the phone again, and I knew he was talking to his wife. He soon hung up, turned to me, and said, "The Sheriff's on his way as soon as he can wrangle up some posse members. They're going to start a search right away. I think it might be best for you guys to go on down into town and maybe get a room. I'm a posse member myself, and we'll keep you in the loop. As soon as we know anything, I'll call you."

Gabby didn't want to leave. She was worried that Lizzie would return during the night, and with no one there would still be in danger. But Gus said they wouldn't leave the house unmanned during the night, so she finally agreed to leave.

I got us a room in town, and it was a long night, one I don't want to repeat. We were both worried sick about Lizzie, but I could also tell that Gabby had been completely traumatized, and I knew she needed help. I knew that my consolations weren't going to be enough to help her regain her sense of security. Her whole world had been turned upside down, and I kicked myself for not going out there earlier.

Actually, I kicked myself even harder for not listening to my gut. After reading the diary I found in the apartment, I should've shut the whole thing down.

We heard nothing at all that night, and the next day was even more difficult, for though Gus did check in, they'd found no trace of our missing daughter.

Finally, Gus called and said a helicopter was scouring the area looking for Lizzie, and he was sure they would find her. He'd stayed up at the house during the night with another posse member, and all had been quiet. They'd left the door unlocked, hoping Lizzie would return, but she hadn't.

Gabby and I spent the next day in the motel room, me going out only to get food. I wanted to go help with the search, but Gabby was such a wreck I didn't dare leave her.

Gus showed up at our room that evening, unfortunately bearing no news, but at least it wasn't bad news. They'd seen absolutely neither hide nor hair of Lizzie, and they'd even had a couple of search dogs out, who'd found no trace of her, not a scent anywhere.

It was beginning to be rather mysterious, and the sheriff and his posse weren't sure what to do next. The helicopter had been out all day searching. It was thick timber with lots of deadfall, so they didn't think Lizzie could've gone far. It was likely she would've heard them as they combed the area and done something to draw attention to herself, but she hadn't.

Gus looked exhausted, but was going to spend another night up at the house, along with another posse member. I can't begin to tell you how grateful we were to these dedicated people, searching for someone they didn't even know.

In the meantime, Gabby had retreated into herself, refusing to talk except for answering basic questions. And the longer all this went on, the more desultory I felt. I was responsible for all this.

What if they never found Lizzie? I could never live with myself. And what would we do with the house now? I knew one thing, Sue would not be our agent when we sold it, which we would.

Imagine my surprise, no, my shock, when someone knocked on our door and I opened it to see Lizzie standing there. I thought for a moment I was looking at a ghost, at something impossible, but when I heard Gabby squeal, I knew she was real.

Gus stood behind her, and he told me he'd just found her on the edge of town a few moments before. Her clothes were torn and she was covered with scratches and exhausted, but otherwise, she was fine—well, at least physically, for I knew the experience had taken a huge toll mentally.

I wanted to know what had happened, but she didn't want to talk about it. Because she was dehydrated and shaky, we decided it would be good to take her to the hospital, even though the nearest one was an hour away. I thanked Gus and told him we would be in contact.

Gabby spent the night with Lizzie in her hospital room, and they released her the next day.

I put them both on a plane home, then pondered what my next step should be concerning the house. I no longer cared what Gabby or Lizzie had to say about it, though I knew they would agree that it was time to get rid of it.

After spending a lot of time on the phone with my son Kevin, he and I came up with a plan. We agreed it would be unethical to try to sell the place without telling the buyer what had gone on, and the odds of anyone wanting to buy a place like that would be very slim. His plan was not totally painless financially, but it would work.

When I got back, I called Gus and asked if he would again go up with me to the house. He generously agreed to.

I was nervous driving up there, Gus following me in his truck in case we came upon another felled tree, and when we finally got there, I could tell he also was shaken. Later, when it was all over and done, he confided in me that he hadn't really completely believed his grandfather, but he did now.

He helped me gather up Gabby and Lizzie's personal things, as well as a few things I'd been told to bring back. This took a couple of hours, and I can tell you, we were both completely on edge, keeping an eye on things outside. I knew Gus was armed, which helped some.

When we were finally done, I took one last look at the house. It was still just as beautiful as ever with its fine furnishings and nice paintings, someone's dream house, though the dream had turned into a nightmare for us.

I was conflicted, for I would never be back, and yet it was still as beautiful and idyllic as before.

"What are you going to do with the place?" Gus asked.

"Well," I answered, "Considering how much you've helped us, my wife and I have decided you and your wife can have your pick of the furnishings. In fact, you can have everything here, and what you don't want, maybe you can sell. We're going to make a sizable donation to your sheriff and his posse as a thank you, and maybe you and your wife will find the stuff here a token of our gratitude."

Gus looked surprised, but I could tell he was interested. I continued, "My son has contacted the park superintendent, and we're going to donate the land and buildings to them for a research station. That parcel should've been part of the park in the first place. We'll get a major tax write-off, and yes, they do know what happened here, and this actually made them even more interested, because they've heard lots of rumors about Bigfoot in the park, and they're hoping that by being here they can maybe verify this. If they could prove that Bigfoot actually existed, it would be a major benefit to these creatures and grant them protection."

Gus looked amused, then said, "My grandfather would be all for that. One of the reasons he quit up here, other than being scared to death, was that he didn't want to destroy their habitat."

He then added, "You know, after I picked up your daughter, she shared a little of what happened when she fled the house. She's a survivor and very gutsy. She said the only way she got away from the Bigfoot was by climbing a really big tree. It apparently didn't see her and kept going. She stayed up there all night, then the next day, she headed straight down the mountain to town. She got cliffed up in a couple of places, but finally made it back. If she was my kid, I'd be very proud."

"That's interesting," I replied. "I haven't had a chance to ask her about it, but you know, I find it really sad that she was in Yellowstone National Park and never got to really see it. I hope she'll come back someday and not let all this deter her. Everyone should see Old Faithful at least once in their life."

Gus just shook his head. "She may not have actually seen the park," he said. "But she's seen things in the park nobody else has ever seen, myself included."

We laughed nervously and headed back down the hill.

3

THE VISION QUEST

I met Christian along the Yellowstone River down near the little town of Emigrant, Montana at what's called the Emigrant Fishing Access. I'd stopped there to check out the boat ramp, thinking I might have some drift-boat clients the next day, and I wanted to see how high the river was running.

Christian was an elderly gentleman who told me he had nothing better to do than come up from his home in Jackson, Wyoming and fish the Yellowstone River every summer. I was intrigued when he told me he'd been a ranger for many years in the park, knowing he had to have some good stories.

He indeed had a special affinity for the area, and I'll let him tell you why in his own words. —Rusty

My name is Christian, and when I tell people I went on a vision quest (which I don't tell many), they always look puzzled, since I'm obviously not Native American, with my red hair and green eyes. Vision quests are a spiritual thing, and I'm also not very spiritual, so those who know me well are even more puzzled.

But I did go on one, and it catapulted my life into a very signifi-
cant change of direction, which is partly what a vision quest is all
about, I guess. In fact, I saw more on that vision quest than I ever
wanted to see, and it changed me profoundly.

But let's start at the beginning, and hopefully it will make more
sense.

I was going to school in my home state of Colorado, working on
an advanced degree in Anthropological Linguistics. Yes, I know it's a
mouthful, but it's basically the study of languages and how they
interact with culture.

One of my profs was an expert in the Crow language, having
worked with the tribe for years, and I decided she would be a good
advisor. I could learn about the Crow Indians up in Montana and
maybe even get to do some fieldwork there. It would be very prestigious to work with her in terms of a future career.

The Crow call themselves the Apsáalooke, and a huge mountain
range named after them runs right through Yellowstone National
Park, the Absarokas, pronounced Ab-sork-as.

Yellowstone was once their traditional summer home, but now
they live on a reservation on the other side of the mountains, south of
Billings, Montana. Their sacred mountains are the Pryor Range.

OK, so after taking all the required first-year grad classes, it was
almost summer, and I needed something to do. I talked with my advisor, Dr. Calder, and she told me there might be some grant money
available to do some fieldwork up at the Crow Agency, and she would
look into it.

I can't tell you how excited I was when she called and said the
Crow would like for someone to come up to the rez and help work on
a Crow dictionary.

I spent that summer studying the Crow language with some of
the elders, helping create a written dictionary for the tribe. The Crow
are a very unified group and value their language and culture,
working to preserve it. Because they didn't fight the invading whites,
they were treated a bit better and were able to keep their tribal cohe-
sion better than other groups.

It was a great summer, and I was too soon back in school, but I then got to spend a second summer with the Apsáalooke. By then, I'd made a few Crow friends.

But by the end of that second summer, things were beginning to change for me. It's hard to describe, but I was feeling more and more alienated from my own culture.

I found myself reluctant to go back to school, even though it would be my last year and I would then get my graduate degree and hopefully a real job, maybe as an assistant prof somewhere.

Now, this isn't all that uncommon in the world of anthropologists and field linguists. There have been many who defected and didn't come back home, choosing instead to live with their adopted people.

In fact, a fellow grad student, Michael, had done the exact same thing the year before and made the Sioux reservation at Standing Rock his home. For all I know, he's still there, though I have no idea how he's making a living. A lot of Native Americans live in poverty.

But I finally did go back home to Colorado, though reluctantly. I got my degree and was now a real linguist, even though when I told people (which I rarely did), they usually just asked how many languages I spoke. I never felt like explaining that linguistics is actually the scientific study of languages, not learning how to speak them.

It was now early summer, and even with my new degree, I had no job prospects. A friend offered me a summer job working in his greenhouse growing flowers, and I took it, since it was that or starve.

Even though working in a greenhouse was fairly pleasant, I found myself daydreaming all the time, riding with my Crow friends across the tall grasses, free and happy. The Crow are part of the plains horse culture, and while I was there I'd learned to ride.

I became more and more unsettled. I missed the reservation, even though I realized these were not my people nor my culture, and I really didn't belong there. But I knew I didn't belong where I was, either, and it all left me feeling more and more ungrounded and depressed.

And to top it off, I realized I was doing nothing with my degree. Even though I'd applied for jobs at several universities, everything came back negative. It seemed that the only place I'd been that appreciated my knowledge was the Crow Agency.

There was still a lot of work to be done there. Could they possibly hire me on somehow? I knew the tribe didn't have much money, but I really didn't need much to survive, especially on the rez, since there's basically no place to spend money there anyway. It was worth a try.

Two weeks later, in late August, I was on my way to Crow Agency, Montana. They would provide housing plus $150 a week, which seemed like a fortune, since I really didn't need much. In exchange, I would continue to work on their dictionary, as well as develop a grammar they could use to teach Crow to the young kids.

And if things worked out, there was a possibility in the future that they would create the position of tribal linguist. The tribe had a paid archaeologist, so why not? It was just a matter of money.

I'll never forget how excited I was driving up the interstate through Wyoming, on past the site of the Battle of Little Big Horn, then taking the exit to Crow Agency. It was a beautiful late-summer day, with big puffy clouds in a deep blue sky, and I couldn't have been happier.

Little did I guess that I would soon be driving back down that same freeway in the opposite direction, eager to get back to Colorado and a new life.

I was given an old rundown house on the edge of town to live in, and I knew I would need to work on it a bunch before winter came if I wanted to stay warm. The doors needed weatherstripping, and two windows were cracked to where a good wind would blow right through them, and I knew the area had plenty of wind.

The inside had mouse droppings all over and the fridge didn't work, but none of it was anything I couldn't deal with.

I was just happy to be there, and my friends greeted my return with a big clean-up party, helping me get the house ready. One brought an old recliner, and another brought a wooden table he'd made for me.

All in all, I felt pretty special. I was there for a purpose, and that purpose was appreciated by most of the people, even though I was an outsider.

One thing I learned from this, in spite of being an outsider, is that people are the same, more or less, and we all have the same basic wants and needs, and one of those needs is feeling like we belong somewhere.

But I eventually realized that no matter how much I wanted to be part of the Apsáalooke Nation, my cultural background would always hold me to a different way of viewing the world, and I would never fully assimilate to their ways.

I settled in pretty quickly, happy to be there, and was soon busy working on the Crow dictionary. Several elders had agreed to work with me, understanding the importance of the language being documented, as it had words and ways of expressing things that English didn't have, ways that helped preserve Crow culture.

I would sit with a different elder for an hour or two every day, rotating between them so they didn't get too tired, trying to figure out how they said different things in Crow.

Interpretation isn't an easy thing to do, as languages aren't perfect matches. For example, if I held up a picture of a running horse and asked the word for it, I could get *iichíile*, the word for a horse, or maybe instead I'd get the word for the motion a horse makes when running, or even the word for the type of wealth one has when they have a lot of horses. It can be a very difficult and exacting process to know which is which.

In addition, Crow is a tone language, and the tone in which a word is spoken, whether high, medium, or low, helps determine the meaning.

Anyway, I got to know several elders very well, and they would ask about my own culture, as the Crow are a very intelligent and curious people.

I would tell them stuff about where I grew up and what college was like and that kind of thing. One of the elders was a guy I'll call Samuel Old Elk, though I've changed his name for this, as I'm not sure he would've wanted people to know who he was.

Sam was a super nice guy, very humble and considered one of the spiritual elders of the tribe. He and I were getting to be very close, and he reminded me of my own grandfather, who had died when I was a teen.

Well, one day, Sam and I were sitting out on some lawn chairs in his backyard when he asked me why I wanted to live in Crow Agency. Why was I living there in poverty when I could be back with my own people, living better and making more money?

I'm an honest guy and pretty open, so I shared with him how I'd found the Crow philosophy to be much more like my basic way of thinking. They were non-materialistic, respected nature, and valued family and experience more than things.

Sam listened carefully, nodding his head in agreement, then surprised me by saying, "If you want to be Apsáalooke, you have to go on a vision quest. It's something all our young men do."

"A vision quest? I thought that was a Lakota Sioux thing," I replied.

Sam grimaced. The Lakota had been enemies of the Crow for as long as anyone knew.

He said, "It's something we all do because it benefits us all equally. Most whites don't know what it's for, so they don't know enough to benefit, even if they try to do it. They don't have the respect and knowledge you need."

"Why would I be any different?" I asked.

"Because you've expressed a desire to be different. You're a searcher, and you need a vision quest to know who you are. Besides, you speak our language, maybe like a baby, but nonetheless, you know the basics."

I was silent for awhile. I'd heard that vision quests could get pretty uncomfortable, and I'm not just referring to the fasting, but to the fact that some questers would actually pierce themselves. It didn't sound like much fun, but then, anytime you're dealing with trying to find yourself, it's usually painful on some level, or so I figured.

Finally, I said, "How would I get the knowledge I need to make a vision quest work? I don't know the Crow ways."

Sam said, "I'll teach you. I never had children, as my wife died young, and I never remarried. I'm 89 years old. I'll teach you, and when you come back from the quest with your new name, you will be my relation. Go home and sleep on it."

It sounded hard, and I wondered later if Sam hadn't been trying to kill me. But if I did go, I would come back with a new name, one that would come to me on the quest. And even though I knew I would never be a true Crow, having an Apsáalooke name would be pretty cool.

All the rest of that day, I thought about having a new name, as if it would make me a new person. And who knew what kind of vision-quest name I would get? Maybe mine would be Gray Wolf or Lone Bear or Flying Eagle.

But I knew I was romanticizing things. One of the older guys in the tribe had came back from his quest with the name Two Days. It had come to him on his third day out, and it was his name from then on.

And another had, believe it or not, come back with the name Belly Button, and he was a very respected tribal member. Apparently, your vision quest name could be anything, its true meaning known only to you.

The very next day, I met with Sam, and he began teaching me about the vision quest. It was not something to take lightly, he emphasized, for some never returned from their quests. They weren't prepared, and the Nirumbee or Awwakkulé were angry and had killed them.

Great! Sam had just added a new danger to the whole thing. The Nirumbee were also called the Little People and were two-foot tall beings with sharp teeth who generally disliked humans and would steal your stuff or tie knots in your hair, or even kill people they didn't like. But occasionally the Nirumbee would help you, but usually only during a vision quest.

The only sure way to pacify the Nirumbee was to leave them tobacco, which they apparently loved, and the Crow would often leave sprinklings of it everywhere when they went to the mountains to collect berries and turnips or to hunt.

"Don't worry," Sam said. "You will take lots of tobacco, and they will like you. You have a good heart, and they sometimes show themselves as lone animals. If you sit quietly, unafraid, they will give you a blessing."

"They've been here forever," Sam continued, "And can be our friends. You must tell them you respect their presence, and then they will respect yours. You mind your business and they will mind theirs. You destroy things, and they will destroy you."

I asked Sam how I would know what my new name was. He replied, "The name is important, but the real reason is to connect with your spirit animal, your guardian spirit. Sometimes a Little Person will lead you to another world where you are introduced to your spirit animal and receive its power."

I went back to my house feeling unsettled. I didn't think I was ready for all this, and I wasn't sure I ever would be. It seemed to cross over into a world I was totally unfamiliar with, a world I was actually afraid of, a world my rational side didn't really believe existed.

And I knew that a big part of such things was belief. Without belief, there was no point in going through with it. And I also had the feeling that what Sam was doing might not be acceptable to the other elders, sharing what were basically tribal secrets.

But Sam was getting more and more excited about being my mentor, and our dictionary studies had completely stopped as he instead took on the task of educating me about Crow ways and beliefs.

One day, while sitting in his back yard eating some watermelon I'd brought, Sam said, "I think you're almost ready. If you don't go soon, the mountains will close up and you won't be able to get into them because of the snows."

It was the end of September, and I'd been missing the displays of gold aspens that are part of the beauty of autumn in Colorado, maybe even feeling a little homesick.

"But we have a problem," Sam continued. "I've talked with the others, and they don't want you going into the Place Where They Fast."

"Where's that?" I asked.

"It's a well-known vision-quest location in the Pryors, also called Castle Rocks. Our famous leaders Two Leggings and Plain Feather fasted there, as well as Plenty Coups. He had a vision there."

I wasn't surprised at the news that some didn't want me in their sacred places, for I knew not everyone thought I should be part of the tribe. I'd had a couple of my friends report that some of the people didn't think it was appropriate. I didn't want to be disrespectful.

"Where else can I go?" I asked.

"I don't know," Sam replied dejectedly. "They don't want you in the Pryors. They think the Little People will get angry at everyone. In fact, they don't want you to go anywhere on the reservation. But there's another place where many go—Awaxaawapìa Pìa, the Crazies."

I knew of the Crazy Mountains, and legend has it they were named by the early explorers because the natives went up there to go crazy, which is how they perceived vision quests. In some way, it was beginning to sound crazy to me, too.

Sam finished his watermelon, then said, "We'll begin with a puri-fying sweat bath, then we'll do an *ise* or bear-root smudging. This takes away the human smell so the spirits aren't afraid of you."

I found this a bit ironic, seeing how afraid I was becoming of the Little People.

"You will then go to your quest place and fast for four days with no food or water, or even longer if needed."

Sam had it all planned out, but I wasn't sure where my quest place would be. He told me to come back the next day and he would tell me exactly where to go, as he wanted to pray more about it.

I returned the next day, figuring I'd soon be headed to the Crazies, but instead, Sam informed me I should go to a place revealed to him in a vision.

"I was told that you should go to one of our old places, a place we used before the whites came, in our old traditional land. None of the young men go there anymore, as it's too far and hard to get to, but the spirits told me that, because you aren't one of us, you must prove yourself."

I felt a bit hurt that not only were some of the young men not accepting me, but now even the spirits seemed doubtful. I laughed at the thought—it seemed I was beginning to believe, after all. I now wanted more than anything to prove myself.

"Where is it?" I asked. "I'll go tomorrow."

Sam sighed. "It's in *Awaxaawe Báaxxioo*, the Pointed Mountains, also called the Absarokas, in Yellowstone National Park. It's difficult to get to. You will climb to the top of Eagle Peak, the highest point in the park."

He looked thoughtful, then continued. "It will be very difficult. You will have a quest like the ancients had. This was the place where the most troubled went long ago."

"Troubled?"

"Those who wanted and needed guidance the most, who wanted the most strength. If you come back with a name, you will be respected by everyone."

It was nearly dark now, the sunset faded to a dull red, the crickets chirping in the grasses. Sam and I sat in silence.

Finally, he said, "You don't have to go. It's no honor lost. You're not a Crow."

"I know," I replied. "I feel like I should do it, though. Maybe if for no other reason than to see if I can figure out where I belong."

Sam was again silent, and I felt a little hurt that he didn't reassure me that I belonged there, but I actually wasn't sure myself if it was true.

"You can go day after tomorrow. Tomorrow we'll have the sweat bath and smudging. But after that, you can't eat or drink, and it will take you some time to get to Eagle Peak. If you turn around, it's OK."

I now started feeling like Sam had little confidence that I could do this. It seemed discriminatory, that I should have such a hard task just because I wasn't Crow. But on the other hand, because I wasn't part of the tribe, doing something so difficult would prove to them that I was serious.

I stood and said, "I'll be back in the morning. I want to get an early start."

I wasn't sure where we would go for the sweat bath and all that, but I would be ready to leave immediately afterwards. From that point on, the clock would be ticking—no food or water.

At home, I pulled out my old road atlas and found Yellowstone, then after much looking, located Eagle Peak.

I was shocked! It was over 200 highway miles just to the trailhead! It would take me hours to drive there, plus the top of the peak was another 20 miles, and all without food and water. I didn't stand a chance. I'd be weak before I even got there.

It would take me the whole first day just to get to the trailhead, then another day to climb the peak. Two days to get there, and another two days to learn my name, hopefully, so that would be around four days, though it would take another two to get back.

From what I could gather, four days seemed the average time for a vision quest, probably because one couldn't go without water much longer and survive. I could take some food and water in a pack with me and eat and drink on the way back down. Hopefully, I could manage that.

I then saw on the map that Eagle Peak was at an altitude of 11,358 feet. How could I possibly climb that high after hiking a good 20 miles or more, especially with no food or water?

I was discouraged, to say the least. Maybe I wasn't cut out to be part of the Crow people and didn't have what it takes. After all, the vision quest was a very old tradition with them, and the young men had been conditioned to it both mentally and physically since birth, kind of like some whites are conditioned to go to college and be financially successful.

I'd gone to college, but the financial part had eluded me, and what made me think I could successfully pull off a vision quest? I thought about it, knowing that even the terms I'd framed it in, as it being something to pull off, were wrong. It wasn't something one pulls off, like good grades in a class or a bank robbery or something. I felt disrespectful and even more doubtful.

I called one of my good Crow buddies, Carlson, and told him what was going on. He was surprised, but agreed to drive me to the trailhead and take my car back to Crow Agency, as I didn't want to leave it sitting there.

Well, Sam and I went ahead with the ceremony the next day, and everything after that was pretty much a blur, except for certain moments that stand out in crystal-clear clarity.

All I remember was a long drive down to Cody, neither me nor Carlson saying a word, then driving past Pahaska Teepee, Buffalo Bill's old place, and finally to the Eagle Creek campground.

There, Carlson left me with my daypack containing some food, a warm coat, a headlamp, and a pouch containing lots of dried tobacco leaves that Sam had gathered in the Pryor Mountains.

There were only a couple of tents at Eagle Creek campground, probably because it was now early October, and nobody seemed to be around, probably out hiking.

I paused, leaning against a post, trying to gather myself. I was getting ready to climb a high peak in the massive Absaroka Range in Yellowstone, a place where winter comes early and is long and hard, and I was going to do it without any water or energy source except my own fat, of which I didn't have much to spare.

It was evening, and I had no tent or sleeping bag, though I did at least have a warm coat. The thought of where I would spend the night didn't even cross my mind.

For some reason, starting out near dark seemed perfectly normal, and in retrospect, I think the ceremony and long ride had served to completely disorient me.

I had started to accept the oncoming hardship much like a bear must accept its oncoming hibernation, something inevitable over which you have no control, and I'd kind of kicked into autopilot.

The problem is, autopilot can kill you in the wilderness, for that's when you need your wits and senses the most. And October is one of the most dangerous times to be around bears, for they're in hyperphagia, that insatiable state when they're trying to take in as many calories as possible for hibernation.

I'd studied the map, and I knew to simply stay on the Eagle Pass trail, following Eagle Creek for about 18 miles. I would cross several small tributaries and eventually come to a wide area called Eagle Creek Meadows, then I would enter a small valley and start up the switchbacks of Eagle Creek Pass.

Once on top of the pass, I would go to the west a short distance, following the ridgeline, then climb up Eagle Mountain.

It all sounded so easy, so idyllic, a nice autumn day hike, though a bit strenuous.

As I walked along the trail, the shadows lengthened, and the gurgling of Eagle Creek seemed to get louder. It was a beautiful place, but all I could think of was Sam's parting words:

"Eagle Peak is a worthy mountain. It's close to the spirits, and you will be able to see Plenty Coups Peak. Remember, you're a part of all these things. You will sacrifice your human wants and needs, and in exchange, the Creator will answer your prayers. Do not hurry home."

Do not hurry home. Was there some hidden meaning in his words? Or was he just advising me to take my time and be sure I got what I needed from the quest.

I paced myself, thinking that if I walked around three miles an hour, a normal pace, it would take me at least six hours to get to the top of the pass. Even though the days were still pretty long, it would be pitch dark by the time I arrived, and there was no way I could climb the peak in the dark.

I'd read some about Eagle Peak and knew the summit was guarded by unbroken cliff bands of breccia, chunks of rock cemented together that make for difficult climbing, as well as a lava tube that you had to crawl through.

The breccia was the remnant of the violent volcanic activity that had formed the Absarokas, some 40 or 50 million years before the Yellowstone hotspot had erupted.

As the trail got harder and harder to see, I decided that once I got there, I would just sit tight on the ridge until it got daylight again, then climb the peak.

I felt a sense of urgency, like time was of the essence, which in a sense, it was, as I had a limited amount of stamina with no food or water. Once on top, after learning my name, I could eat and drink and things would get easier, at least in theory, assuming I was still alive, then I could come back down.

I hadn't had anything to drink since the ceremony that morning, and I was already getting thirsty, the sound of the creek running nearby getting more and more torturous with each step.

As I walked along, I wondered what my new name would be. Walks Too Slow, I thought, or Stumbles in Dark.

The last lingering rays of light were soon gone, leaving me to silently find my way along a trail leading through what had become a mysterious landscape of shadows, forest on one side and creek on the other.

The moon soon rose, three-quarters full, and I found that if I turned my headlamp off and let my eyes acclimate to the dark, I could actually see better, the trail stretching before me like a long dark ribbon.

Several times I stopped, listening as animals on the trail ahead of me crashed into the forest, surprised. I was feeling pretty spooked myself.

I had to cross two shallow streams, the largest being Cloudburst Creek, for which I used a big stick I'd found along the trail to balance myself. I had to use my headlamp to not twist my ankle on the rocks, but I turned it back off after each crossing.

I'd been hiking for hours when I finally approached the base of the pass. It was now pitch dark, the stars hanging above me like a cloud of fireflies frozen in time. I knew that once I got on top of the peak, the night sky would be even more spectacular, but I first had to make it up the steep switchbacks of Eagle Pass. It was starting to get cold, and I could see my breath when I switched on my headlamp.

It was now more difficult to see the trail, so I turned on my head-lamp again so as not to inadvertently go tumbling down the mountainside. I would turn it on and scope out the trail, then turn it off to save batteries, though I'd brought extra. I did this every hundred feet or so, slowly working my way upwards.

I kept seeing shadows as if something was on the trail far ahead, but when I would get closer, there would be nothing there. I decided it was deer or elk or even bears using the trail. Whatever it was, it spooked me even more.

I was lagging, tired, and though I wasn't particularly hungry, the thirst was always there, driving me onwards, for I knew I could drink only after the quest ended.

I stumbled on a rock and almost fell to my knees, the walking stick I'd picked up for the stream crossings the only thing saving me. I felt a hint of bitterness, for if I'd been allowed to go into the Pryor Mountains or the Crazies, I would be there by now, not climbing some impossible mountain. It wasn't my fault I hadn't been born a Crow. Why did I have to do so much more to prove myself?

I truly was in the heart of the wilderness, for this section of the park was near the Thorofare, the most remote place in the contiguous United States. Only the most dedicated backpackers came into the Thorofare, as it's hard to access, but it's beautiful, famous for its solitude and wildlife.

It wasn't long before things became exponentially more difficult, and I knew I'd lost the trail. I turned around, backtracking, but after awhile, I knew it would be impossible to find it in the dark.

I had two choices: I could stop where I was and wait for morning and then try to find the trail, or I could continue upwards. The smart thing to do would be to wait until I could see, but I'd studied the map carefully, and I knew if I continued I would reach the ridge that led to Eagle Peak.

I was following the rocky drainage of a small unnamed creek, and it didn't take long to realize I was definitely taking the hard way. My new name would be Loses Trail.

And sure enough, I was soon climbing through loose scree, far from any trail. Several times I almost fell, my walking stick again being all that saved me. And soon I had to negotiate small cliff bands, scrambling up some and around others in the dark, trying not to think about what a twisted ankle would mean out here all alone in late autumn.

I continued upward, driven by the fear that I would fail and all would be lost. For some reason, the farther I went, the more I felt the need to prove myself, even though there was no one there to prove myself to. But maybe that's really what I was there for, to prove myself to myself, not to become a Crow, for I knew I would never really be one of them anyway.

I knew I had to be nearing the top of the pass when I suddenly heard the sound of rocks clattering down. There was something above me.

Soon, I could hear what sounded like more and more rocks coming down with a roar. Whatever it was, it had triggered a rock avalanche, and it sounded like I was directly in its path!

I turned on my light just in time to see a cloud of dust and rocks roaring past me. If I'd been standing a mere ten feet to that side I would've been hit! As it was, a few smaller rocks landed nearby, a couple of small ones hitting my shins.

I sat down, shaken. My new name would be Crushed by Rocks. What had triggered the avalanche? Probably bighorn sheep, I decided.

I was soon back on my feet, hoping to reach the ridge by dawn, as I could feel the cold sapping my strength. I had to keep moving.

After another hour or two of fighting my way up the steep loose rock I paused, as something felt different and the light had changed. Turning on my headlamp, I realized I'd come to a large snowfield.

Should I continue on? The walking would be much easier, even though somewhat steep, but would I fall in a crevasse? I decided to continue on, but more carefully, using my stick to probe ahead.

I wallowed a bit in the snow, as it was steep, but suddenly my instincts told me to stop. Shining my light outward, it revealed nothing but space, and I realized I was now on the ridge.

I'd made it! I would stop here and rest until there was enough daylight to continue on up Eagle Peak.

My throat was now dry to where I could barely swallow. I thought of the water in my pack and wanted nothing more than to have just one sip, or even a handful of the nearby snow.

I had no idea what time it was but figured it must be near dawn, for my pace coming up in the dark had been agonizingly slow. No longer moving, I started getting cold, so I took my coat from my pack and slipped it on.

I was soon fast asleep, even though I was uncomfortable lying on hard rock. At one point, I woke and swore there were lights shining around me, but I soon fell back asleep.

When I awoke a second time, the sun was shining directly in my eyes, though the valley below was still draped in shadows. It took some time before I realized that I was indeed on the ridge leading to Eagle Peak. If I remembered the map correctly, the ridge was over 10,000 feet high.

Since leaving Eagle Creek Campground at 6500 feet, I'd hiked 3,500 feet, all in the dark. It was an incredible feat, at least for me, especially with no food or water. But at the time, I thought nothing of it. It was all a blur.

I watched as the sun gradually opened up the immense landscape below, one that stretched from thick forest to mountaintop and beyond. I was looking at only a small portion of Yellowstone, and it made me begin to realize how totally vast it really was.

The Crow had hunted here for thousands of years, gathered plants, and used the geysers as fasting places. They knew the area well, even though the early whites had tried to make it sound like the natives were afraid of the place in a campaign to take it from them. And to the Crow, supernatural beings were everywhere here, in this sacred place.

And as my gaze took in the vast scene below me, I realized I'd made a huge mistake, for above me and to the east was Eagle Peak, not to the west, where it should have been had I come up the pass.

On this side, the peak was guarded by thick cliff bands, too high and steep for one to negotiate without ropes. There was no way I was going to climb it without descending the way I'd come and then climbing back up the pass. It was an impossible task, and I wasn't even sure I had enough strength to climb it had I come up the right side.

I sat back down, depressed. A peregrine falcon whizzed over me, carrying what looked like a small rodent, probably on its way to feed its chicks.

Some vision quest. I didn't even have enough competence to find the peak I was supposed to climb. My new name would be Incompetent White Boy.

But after awhile, I realized that I was looking at things the wrong way. I had already achieved a very difficult goal, and in the dark, no less!

Looking back down the way I'd come I realized it had only been sheer luck that had led me up the route I'd taken, for most of the way was marked by inaccessible cliffs, small glaciers, and even a couple of waterfalls. And to top things off, I'd done it with no food or water and narrowly escaped being smashed by a rock avalanche.

I now turned and looked again at Eagle Peak. Luck or no, there was virtually no way I could climb it from this side. I turned and looked further west, where the long narrow ridge I was on ended in Mount Humpheys. I entertained the thought of climbing it instead, but the ridge was intimidating, as were more cliff bands that made the mountain look as unclimbable as Eagle Peak.

But ahead of me, stretching out to the south, was a lower ridge that led to Table Mountain. I'd studied this ridge on my map back at Crow Agency, thinking it might be a quicker way off Eagle Peak than going down the backside of Eagle Pass.

The ridge to Table Mountain looked narrow but negotiable, although this side of Table Mountain looked steep and inhospitable. But maybe I could angle around and climb it from the other side.

As I stood looking out, it dawned on me how totally driven I was to continue with the vision quest, in spite of my big SNAFU. What was pushing me? Did I really want to be a part of the Crow people that badly? I was beginning to feel somewhat ambivalent about it— was something else driving me?

Putting my pack back on, ever mindful of the bottle of water inside, I set off on what would become a spectacular walk along the narrow spine leading to Table Mountain, along places barely wide enough to place one's feet.

And later, when I looked at photos of it, I was amazed I'd done it, for no way would I have even tried it if I'd been in my right mind. All I recall is the delusional thought that if I fell, the snow far below would save me from harm.

I had decided I would go have my vision quest on Table Mountain, for as Sam might say, it, too, was a worthy mountain. In some ways, it was even better than Eagle Peak, for it was the second highest peak in the park and much easier to climb, its south face a gentle slope blanketed by green tundra.

For some reason, about halfway to my new goal, I turned and looked back. Eagle Peak stood behind me, an imposing sight, and I was glad I had screwed up and wouldn't be climbing it after all.

But as I stood looking back, the rising sun backlighting it, I felt a sense of doom rise in me unlike any I'd ever felt before or since, for I could see several dark figures on the summit, and even from that distance, I could tell they weren't human because of their size and bulk.

At first I thought they might be large rocks backlit by the sun, but when they moved, I knew they were alive. And somehow, I knew they were some of the malevolent spirits that Sam had told me to be wary of. These were not Little People, appeased by the tobacco in my pack, but were some kind of giants, some kind of evil spirits embodied in flesh and bone.

Don't tell me why—maybe it was my muddled state of mind—but I was convinced they were waiting for me, and they had to be able to see me. Standing on that backbone ridge, I was as exposed as one can get.

I shivered, turned, and began making my way as fast as I could towards Table Mountain. I could climb down its more gentle slopes and follow the creek to Yellowstone Lake, where surely I would find someone—hikers, fishermen, or even a ranger.

I nearly fell several times, my feet uncertain on the narrow rubbly ridge, but I could finally better see the rocky mass of the mountain. I was crestfallen—there was no way I could climb it without somehow circumnavigating more cliffs.

After studying things for a moment, ever mindful of being seen, I could see the peak was all but inaccessible from this side, as a deep chasm broke the ridge line. In addition, this whole side was a high cliff, and there was no way I was going to climb it without ropes. It was like Eagle Peak, climbable only from one side.

The ridge I was on had now widened and began to drop down into a huge drainage. I climbed down out of view, trying to figure out what to do next.

Part of me wanted to open my pack, drink the water and eat the food, leave the tobacco on a rock as an offering for safe passage, then go down to Yellowstone Lake.

The sun was now overhead, and I was lightheaded, my throat so parched that it was beginning to feel like I had strep throat. But in spite of that, I felt strong enough, and I knew I could be back to the lake by evening, especially if I drank some water. I would just go back to Colorado and forget this entire escapade.

I was obviously starting to hallucinate, seeing the figures on Eagle Peak, and it made me worry about my ability to stay alive. I already felt as if things were becoming marginal.

High above to my left stood a tall volcanic spire called the Watchtower, and I'd read it was the only place in Yellowstone where lynx had been spotted. I saw a small herd of bighorn sheep high above, who turned and disappeared into the rocks as they spotted me.

I started down the slope into the long valley, knowing that it held Trapper's Creek, a small drainage that eventually fed into the Yellowstone River. I was quickly losing altitude, my hopes for a vision quest disappearing in the distance behind me.

Finally, whatever I'd seen high on Eagle Peak didn't seem quite as threatening, and I decided it was time to take a break and take stock of things. I took off my pack and eagerly took out the bottle of water, thinking of how cool and soothing it would feel on my throat.

But something made me hesitate. Was I really and truly ready to give up on the quest? I would return to Sam with no name, a failure, confirming his lack of faith in my abilities to follow the Crow ways. I would have to relinquish my hopes for a job as Crow linguist, for I would be too ashamed to stay there.

I held the bottle of water to my cheek, feeling its coldness, then returned it to the pack. Sam had said I had to go to Eagle Peak, but why was I bound to his advice? Yes, he'd had a vision, but wasn't having a quest somewhere different better than none at all?

I now took out the beautifully beaded tobacco pouch that Sam's wife had made long ago. I'd promised to return it, and I pictured the look of sadness and disappointment on Sam's face when I would hand it to him.

Taking out a pinch of tobacco, its pungent odor filling the air, I carefully rubbed it all over my arms and face, and then placed some on a nearby rock. I would go ahead with the quest, but I would choose a place not quite as close to the spirits, maybe something here in the trees.

I felt calm, as if I could still achieve what I'd set out to do, but on my own terms. I needed to find a suitable place, then I could get on with my quest.

I looked up, motion in the tundra startling me. There was something there! Had the black spirits on Eagle Peak found me?

Whatever it was had disappeared behind a rise, but when it reappeared, I could see it was a huge grizzly digging for tubers, probably a male from its size.

Just when I was sure it hadn't noticed me, it looked up, shook its head, then immediately began running straight towards me. Shocked at how fast it could move, I simply sat there, watching. I had nowhere to run to and felt curiously detached.

Was this one of Sam's *Nirumbee*, one of the Little People who had taken the form of a lone animal and was now going to kill me? I remembered that he'd said I must tell them I respect their presence so they would leave me alone.

"I respect your presence," I said, simply.

A mere 20 feet away, it stopped, snorted, then turned and ran on down towards the creek, leaving me feeling as if I'd just experienced something from another world.

I knew bluff charges by grizzly were fairly common. Had the animal been puzzled by the fact that I smelled like tobacco? Maybe my new name would be Smells Like Tobacco or Confuses Charging Bear.

It was now getting on towards evening, the shadows again lengthening, and I felt the strong urge to get up higher, someplace where I could see out. I knew this was a defensive feeling common to all humans when alone in the wilderness, especially when unarmed.

It was then that I noticed a small cliff right above the creek. It was about 30 feet high, a place where I could see all around.

Climbing up its back side, I was soon on top. It was already getting chilly, though nothing like the previous night up on the ridge, and I was thankful for my warm coat. The thought that I might pass out had occurred to me, and I wanted to stay warm if that should happen.

What I saw next was not something I even vaguely expected, but the thought of it made me feel as if I'd somehow almost been led there, if such things can happen.

The open area on top of the cliff was flat and grassy, and I could see a faint outline of what I recognized to be a vision-quest bed, even though some of the rocks had fallen from the low wall.

For their vision quests, the Crow often stacked rocks into an elongated u-shaped wall that was the right size for a human to recline in. The low walls served as protection from the wind, and these structures were usually built on the edge of precipitous cliffs with drop-offs.

I knew it was Crow because it opened to the east, where Ihkale'axe, the Morning Star, rises. To the Crow, the Morning Star is important to a vision quest because it appears in the sky at the time of night when a person was most likely to receive a vision, that holiest of times when the Creator was closest to the earth. The star Sirius is the Crow Morning Star, not Venus.

I couldn't believe it! After stumbling around and practically killing myself for two entire days, I'd accidentally found exactly where I needed to be, and it was nowhere even close to where I'd been told to go. I wondered if Sam had even actually had a vision. Had he purposely misled me?

I couldn't decide which was worse, the exhaustion, the thirst, or the hunger, but I knew I needed to rest. I got more tobacco from the pouch, sprinkling it all around the vision-quest structure, then placed what was left on a large nearby rock. I then zipped up my coat, pulled the hood around my head, and lay down, my feet towards the opening to the east, just a few feet from the cliff drop-off.

I was too tired to sleep, and I lay there watching the sunset, the clouds to the west turning a brilliant gold, then fading into a dull gray. I wondered if a storm might be brewing as I watched the starry sky open up, looking like millions of bright points hanging just above me.

I felt restless, like something wasn't right, and I suddenly knew exactly what it was. I felt like I was desecrating a sacred space by lying in the vision-quest structure. It seemed disrespectful for me to be there.

I pulled myself up and turned my light on. I would find a place in the nearby trees to rest. I was soon lying under a tree in soft pine needles, though I could still see the structure.

I now heard a yipping in the distance, followed by a chorus of what I knew were coyotes. A deep feeling of contentment took hold of me, a feeling as if I'd finally found my true home, and I soon drifted off into a dreamless sleep.

I woke to a deep darkness, shivering, the sky as black as doom, and I realized the stars and moon were gone, replaced by an ominous bank of low clouds and bone-chilling cold.

I was now very afraid, for it was late autumn, and I knew there was no way I could survive a big storm, especially if it snowed, and this time of year the odds were good it would.

Sitting up, I could tell that a cold wind was beginning to pick up. I shivered, knowing I should've abandoned the quest while it was still light and instead headed on down Trapper's Creek.

I would be at the Cabin Creek Patrol Cabin by now, which was along the trail back to Yellowstone Lake, though it was likely it would be locked up this late in the season.

But I could've broken in and at least stayed warm and dry. I knew that, given the shape I was in, there was no way I could survive any kind of wet weather.

I had to go immediately. I would eat and drink, then use my light to try to make it to the cabin, which I guessed to be about five miles away.

It was the first time that it occurred to me that I might die. It had been almost three days since I'd had food and water. Maybe I should wait until first light, then try to get out, my vision quest ended.

But as the wind picked up, I thought I could hear voices. For some reason, my mind was much clearer now than even before the cleansing ceremony back at Crow Agency, and I knew it was an illusion.

The voices seemed to be getting closer, and though I could hear what sounded like words, they were unintelligible, like a foreign language. I slipped back into the trees, making myself as low to the ground as possible, though I knew no one could see me in this blackest of nights.

I soon could hear the shuffling of feet, and I thought I saw shadows standing by the rock structure.

Now a deep voice said, "Kahée," which I recognized as the Crow word for "hello."

Had they seen me? I said nothing.

Another voice said, "Hilík," which means "Here you are."

I realized now that they were talking to each other, not to me.

"Ítchik daluúom!" said a third voice. "It's good you've come!"

"Where did the little man go? He was just here," said the first voice. "I followed him."

"He can't be far," the second answered. "He's fatigued. He won't last much longer."

I squinted, trying to make out who was there, but all I could see were black shadows.

"He should build a fire," the first one said. "This storm will be very bad. He won't be able to walk out in the deep snow."

For some reason, I got the feeling that they knew exactly where I was. Was it some kind of test? Was it part of the vision quest?

I remembered now what Sam had said, and though he was talking about the Little People, for some reason it seemed appropriate.

Don't worry. You will take lots of tobacco, and they will like you. You have a good heart, and they sometimes show themselves as lone animals. If you sit quietly, unafraid, they will give you a blessing.

Now the third one said, "Christian Wants to be Crow. That's his name. He can reveal himself now that he knows it."

The dark shadow seemed to be looking in my direction. They had to know I was here. The thought filled me with terror.

These were the same creatures I'd seen on Eagle Peak, waiting for me on top, and now they'd found me. And in spite of what Sam had said about them giving me a blessing, I knew it wasn't going to happen, probably because they saw me as an imposter.

I then realized that when you imitate someone's tradition and you don't know what you're doing, there's a danger of something going very wrong. The past three days had all been wrong, and now it was all going to end here.

I could see my body, frozen, lying under deep snow, deep in the remote heart of Yellowstone. And right then, I wanted nothing more than to go home, back to my own people in Colorado.

"Look! Íhchihchia! Sacred tobacco!"

One of the shadows had found the pile on the rock. He seemed amused.

"He thinks we can smoke," he added.

"He needs to give up and go home," another said.

I didn't know if the voices were real or if I was hallucinating, but it didn't matter, they seemed real enough, and they seemed like they wanted me gone. I would've been more than happy to accommodate them, for I wanted nothing more than to leave.

But then, I felt as if a wave rolled over me, a wave of detachment, and somehow I could hear Sam's voice. I knew it had to be my imagination, but it seemed very real.

"Observe and listen, without judgement, simply paying attention. Your voice is silent now, it can rest and be still. Breathe. Know you're safe in the moments to come."

Now the first one said, "Let's kill him."

The second and third laughed menacingly. I was sure they were looking my way, and my hair stood on end, for now I could see they had glowing red eyes.

They were coming towards me when a new voice said, "Leave him alone. He's one of my people."

I couldn't believe it. It was indeed Sam. How had he gotten here? He was too old to hike in. Had someone brought him on horseback? It didn't make sense.

Now the third voice said, "He's not Crow. He doesn't look right."

"He's Crow," Sam repeated.

"Then what's his name?"

"Christian Hides in Trees. You will not touch him."

I tried to take in what had been said, and then I realized, whatever it was, my subconscious or something outside me, it had just given me my new name!

Christian Hides in Trees. I almost laughed out loud. It sounded cowardly, and yet it was so fitting! I felt comfortable in the trees, hidden, and I realized that even as a kid, I loved being in the forest.

When I had free time, I would always head for the timber, the woods, instead of the open fields or rolling hills, sometimes taking a book along to read. I was truly Christian Hides in Trees in more ways than one.

And even though I was faint from hunger and thirst, miles from any kind of help, overwhelmed by what appeared to be Bigfoot spirits, I suddenly felt like the luckiest person on the planet. I now knew what I needed to do.

"Our friend, Christian Hides in Trees, needs to eat and drink," Sam said. "We will now pray and give him a blessing so he can go home."

The clouds must've been thinning a little, for there was enough moonlight that I could now see the silhouettes of the three beings, but I still couldn't see Sam.

The creatures were large and massive, and the wind was blowing their long hair, making it stand out away from their thick bodies. They had to be Bigfoot.

They began chanting in low voices, and it sounded like Crow, but I couldn't make out what they were saying. Soon all was quiet, and I knew they were gone.

"Sam?" I asked quietly, hoping it wasn't a trick and the Bigfoot were still around, hiding.

The only sound was the wind whispering through the trees.

I very quietly reached into my pack and pulled out the bottle of water and silently drank, and I can tell you, never in my life has something tasted so good.

It wasn't a large bottle, and it seemed to just make me thirstier, but I knew I would soon be down by Trapper's Creek and could drink my fill.

I then pulled out some beef jerky and slowly chewed each bite, the sensation of eating seeming foreign. And as new life slowly coursed through me, I thought of how ironic it was to have Bigfoot as my spirit animal.

Wasn't that what had transpired here? Sam or someone had told me that if I sat quietly, unafraid, they would give me a blessing, and that's exactly what it seemed had happened. I'd never heard Sam mention Bigfoot, and I wasn't even sure the Crow people believed they existed.

But it didn't matter, because the wind was again picking up, the temperature was dropping, and I needed to go.

I ate several handfuls of pinon nuts, then stood, grabbed my headlamp, and put on my pack. I had no idea what time it was, but I knew it was a long hike to the ranger cabin, and even further to the edge of Yellowstone Lake.

I had no idea what I would do if there was no one at the cabin, and the odds were good there wouldn't be, this time of year. I might have to hike around the lake, and I knew it was a long way.

Once I met up with the Yellowstone River I would be on the Thorofare Trail, which eventually rounded the lake to Fishing Bridge. I remembered reading it was about 20 miles from Fishing Bridge to the ranger cabin.

I slowly bushwhacked through thick stretches of deadfall, remnants of the big 1988 fire, my light revealing wolf, moose, and elk tracks. It was extremely slow going in the dark, and the air had that heaviness that precedes a big snow.

Once at the edge of Trapper's Creek, I filled my bottle and drank until I could hold no more, then sat and ate more nuts.

I was gradually regaining my energy, and I knew the Bigfoot I'd seen at the vision-quest site had to have been a dream or hallucination, for now my entire outlook had changed, my clarity returning, and the event seemed ludicrous.

Full of food and water, I wanted to sleep, but I knew it was almost morning, for things seemed to be getting lighter, and I could make out low gray clouds overhead. I had to keep going.

And as I walked along, making my way through the willows and rocks along the creek, reveling in the fact that I could now drink, I wondered yet again why I would hear Sam's voice. I had actually doubted his faith in me more than once—was I somehow subconsciously trying to rectify something?

As it started spitting snow, I pulled my hood up, knowing I had to step up my pace. It wasn't long before it was light enough that I could see ahead to where Trapper's Creek merged with the Yellowstone River.

I'd made it to the Thorofare Trail! At least there was now no longer any chance of getting lost, and if I could slog along far enough, I knew I would reach the Cabin Creek Patrol Cabin in just a couple of hours.

At times the trail climbed above the river, and at times it skirted rock cliffs, the river right beside the trail. The Yellowstone was slow and sluggish, its spring runoff long gone into Yellowstone Lake. Something startled down in the willows, and I soon realized it was a moose.

Mindlessly walking, I soon slipped into a Zen-like state, thinking about everything that had happened and still wondering if I was safe from the spirits or Bigfoot or whatever they'd been. I turned often to look behind me, but saw nothing.

It was early afternoon when I realized I had to have passed the cabin. Like all the old Yellowstone backcountry cabins, I knew it set on the edge of a meadow and not next to the trail, not necessarily obvious.

The cabins had been constructed about 16 miles apart, which was considered a reasonable day's travel on horseback, and were built to house rangers on backcountry patrols looking for poachers.

I was crestfallen, for I knew the cabin would provide at the very least a warm shelter. But on the other hand, if it did snow a lot, I risked getting snowbound there, unable to negotiate deep snows without skis or snowshoes. Maybe it was for the best, I thought, trudging on, the food in my pack now gone.

It was almost dark when I finally reached the big grassy meadows that marked where the river entered Yellowstone Lake. The moon, now almost full, rose over the peaks high above, casting shadows on my path.

I felt much better than at any previous time on the trip, but I knew there was no way I could continue on to Fishing Bridge. I would somehow have to hunker down for the night. Maybe I could find a dry place under the trees. I smiled at my new name, Christian Hides in Trees. For some reason, it comforted me.

The wind had died down for the most part, and the clouds seemed to have parted and partially blown over, the snow stopping. The whole place looked like something in a fairy tale, the big pines and spruce trees backlit by the moonlight.

It was then that I heard it. Something big was coming along the trail behind me, making no effort to be quiet.

At that point, I was too tired to even be afraid. If it were the three Bigfoot, then maybe Sam would help me again. If not, then I would have died seeing one of the most beautiful sights in the world, moonlight on the upper Yellowstone.

Something was nearly upon me, and as I jumped back, it snorted. I at first thought it was another moose, but I couldn't believe my ears when I heard a voice say, "Easy, Danny. Who's there?"

Now a powerful light was shining right in my face, and I knew this was no Bigfoot, but a park ranger.

"What are you doing out here?" He asked.

"I'm trying to get out before the storm hits," I answered, stating what was probably the obvious.

The ranger was now down off his horse, still shining his light on me.

"Where's your backpacking gear?"

"I don't have any."

"Do you have a permit? They told me there was nobody in here. Are you hunting?"

I was too tired to answer. He studied me for awhile, then asked to look in my pack. After he handed it back to me, he got back on his horse, told me to put my foot in the stirrup, then pulled me up behind him.

"It's a bit of a ride back, but we'll be out in a few hours. Danny here could walk this trail blindfolded. When we get out, I'll be asking you some questions."

It was a long ride, and several times I went to sleep and almost fell off, but we finally made it to Fishing Bridge, where the ranger unsaddled Danny, fed him some oats and hay, then turned him into a big corral for the night.

I then followed him into a park building, where he asked me all kinds of questions. I told him everything, all about the vision quest and where I'd come up and where I'd gone down, but I didn't tell him about the Bigfoot.

After I was done, he had a pained look on his face, and I knew he was too tired to want to deal with me.

"Look," he said. "It's really late. I'm not usually on the trail after dark, but I had trouble up at the cabin. I went in to button it down for the winter, but the door was twisted off the hinges, and I basically had to rebuild it. Do you have any place to go for the night?"

I nodded my head no, and I knew that, there in the light, I must've looked like a dead man walking.

"The lodge is closed for the season, but I'll see if we can get you into a cabin or something."

Before I knew it, I was fast asleep in the warmest coziest bed I'd ever slept in, after having a nice meal at the Lake Lodge deli, everything else being closed. I slept until noon the next day and would've slept longer, but the ranger came and got me. He was going to Cody, and I needed to go along, as the park would be closing all the roads soon. Before we left, I called Carlson to come and meet me there.

Riding in his patrol pickup, pulling Danny in a horse trailer, I asked the ranger if he was going to give me a ticket for not having a backcountry permit. He laughed and told me it was worth it just hearing me tell about my escapade.

And in the end, on the way to Cody, I did tell him about the Bigfoot. He just nodded his head as if he knew exactly what I was talking about, but didn't say much.

Carlson picked me up, and we went back to Crow Agency, where I packed my stuff and got ready to leave, to go back to Colorado.

But first, I wanted to go see Sam. I needed to tell him my new name and ask him how he'd managed to be at the vision quest structure that night. I knew it was impossible, as he was an old man and there was no way he could get up there, even on horseback. Maybe it had been an elaborate trick and he would come clean, but I suspected it had been an hallucination.

I first went to Carlson's to tell him goodbye. We talked awhile, then I told him that I was on my way to see Sam.

Carlson looked concerned, asking, "Didn't you know? Nobody told you?"

"Told me what?"

"Sam died the day after you left. He just slipped away in his sleep. They took him out into the Pryors for burial."

It took me a long time to process this news. It almost seemed as if Sam had known, and I wondered if that was why he had told me not to hurry home, as he knew he wouldn't be there.

I gave Sam's beaded tobacco pouch to his brother, then left Crow Agency and went back to Colorado, where I eventually got a seasonal job as a park ranger. After a few years of this, it turned into a full-time career position, one that suited me, Christian Hides in Trees, perfectly.

And ironically enough, after ranger stints in other parks, I was offered the position of park ranger in Yellowstone, patrolling, of all places, the Thorofare.

I spent the rest of my career there, horseback patrolling, and I was never once afraid out there, for I knew Sam was watching over me, strange as it may sound. I found it somewhat ironic that my job was to protect the ancestral lands of the Crow when I'd so badly wanted to be one of them.

Did I ever see another Bigfoot? No, but I found tracks more than once, and I heard them howling in the distance, along with their woodknocking.

And my horse, Gus, shied more than once, afraid to go near a particular thicket or wooded area, a horse who was unafraid of moose and even bear.

I love the Thorofare, and if you'd told me when I was up there trying to climb Eagle Peak that I would abandon my job as a linguist to be a park ranger, well, I wouldn't have believed you, because the thought had never occurred to me.

And as for having Bigfoot as my spirit animal, I think about that and just shake my head. It had to have been just an hallucination, and even if it wasn't, I never got the feeling that they would want to have anything to do with me, yet alone give me any special powers. I'm pretty sure I wouldn't want anything to do with them either.

But I do know this one thing: some things are real, and it doesn't matter if you believe in them or not. And to this day, when I think about who I really am, even though I'm now long retired from being a park ranger and go into the forest only on my way to fly fish, I treasure my name of Christian Hides in Trees, for it opened my eyes to what I really wanted to do with my life.

4

THE NIGHT SOUNDS

I met Katie and Dan at, of all places, a silent auction fundraiser for a local charity. I was dropping off two tickets for a fly-fishing lesson that I'd donated, and since I'm not much of one for crowds, I was in a hurry.

The couple had come to my hometown of Steamboat Springs, Colorado on vacation, and ended up being the winning bid on the tickets. They were super nice people, and after the lesson, Katie wanted to know of some good places to do nature sound recordings.

Steamboat has a number of local hot springs, so I took them to visit a few, as well as to a place where the fish are always jumping and making lots of plopping and popping noises.

I wasn't sure about that one, but Katie seemed delighted to be able to record fish jumping, and after she sent me a copy of the recording, I use it to go to sleep on nights when I feel restless—like I felt after she told me the following story. —Rusty

Rusty, I'm what's called a sound producer or recordist, but most people have no idea what that means. But when I tell them I'm one of those people who go out and record those nature sounds that you use for meditation, white noise, and sleeping, they immediately know what I'm talking about.

My recordings run the gamut from the sound of creeks and waterfalls to birdsong, rain, and even things like the calls of coyotes and wolves. In short, if it's something you'd hear in nature, I've recorded it, though I usually stick to ambient sounds, the kind that make you relax.

I mention relaxing because I have an accidental recording that has the opposite effect, which I'll get into here soon.

I have some very sophisticated recording equipment and make 3-D, binaural recordings. This is a method using two microphones which makes it sound like you're actually there. If you use headphones and close your eyes, you really can imagine yourself out in nature.

I don't really understand it, but people like to hear sounds from places they've been to or would like to visit. To me, if you've heard one babbling creek, you've heard them all, but if that creek is in the Tetons or Yosemite, it's way more popular than if it's the little brook out in my backyard, even though they all sound similar.

It's kind of funny, but I've actually done tests on my friends, saying the first sound is something like Granite Creek or Jenny Lake in Teton National Park and the second is some stream or lake in Idaho, and they'll always prefer the Teton one, even if I play the same sound twice. I guess it just depends on which place they'd rather imagine themselves.

The same goes for birdsong. I can tell someone that a recording is of sandhill cranes along the Platte River in Nebraska, or of sandhill cranes in Utah, and they'll always prefer the one in Nebraska, seeing that's where the birds are most iconic.

People ask if I actually make a living doing this, and I have to say yes, I make a good living, and on top of that, I get to be out in places I really enjoy. I've traveled all over the world making recordings. You can buy my recordings on the internet, and I also sell to science and nature museums, educational centers, and even movie producers.

As you can guess from what I said above, my most popular stuff comes from the national parks. There's a catch here, though, as any time you're involved in an activity in a national park that can make money, you have to have a permit, and that can get expensive. On top of that, they don't always let you go where you want, as they regulate traffic during certain times of the year, especially in the spring when the wildlife has babies.

Anyway, I was out recording the sound of elk bugling in the fall in the Tetons, which has a big elk refuge, and it occurred to me that I should do albums of the national parks, just like photographers do. For example, I could make a sound album of the Tetons that would include the elk bugling, coyotes howling, Hidden Falls, Cascade Creek, various songbirds, owls at night—well, you get the picture.

So, I got a permit and went to Teton National Park and recorded a bunch of different sounds, with each recording about 10 minutes long, then put them all together into an album.

It was a big hit. Nature sounds are getting more and more popular as people realize how much they can de-stress you. The album sold to all kinds of people—spa owners, therapists, even psychiatrists. I thought, wow, this is a great way to make a living, going to the national parks and recording nature's music. I felt like I was onto something.

It takes time to put an album like this together. You have to decide where to go and what to record, hopefully places that people will recognize and want to reminisce about, if they've been there. Then you have to come back to the studio and clean everything up and make a master and then upload it to the various sales platforms. I spent part of a year making park albums for the Tetons and the Grand Canyon.

You might wonder what there is to listen to in the Grand Canyon, since you don't have all the waterfalls and rippling brooks like in the mountains, but I have some cool recordings of the wind sighing through trees, raptor calls, condor grunts and snorts, as well as Havasu Falls and some rapids on the Colorado River.

Well, I was trying to hit the most popular parks, so I decided that my next album would be Yellowstone. I would record some of the geysers like Old Faithful, then do Yellowstone Falls, some of the creeks, and things like osprey calls, buffalo, bear, moose, and elk sounds, and maybe even get some wolves howling, if I was lucky.

I had wrapped up my Grand Canyon album in the fall, the same time they close the roads into Yellowstone, so I figured I'd have to wait until spring to get started. There was a possibility that maybe I could go into the Lamar Valley in the winter, as that's the only road open. The Lamar wolf pack hangs out there, and sometimes even the Mollies pack, so maybe I could at least record them.

I booked a nice little cabin in Gardiner, the small town at the north entrance, which was very quiet at that time of year. I would use it as a base while recording everything I could think of in the part of the park that was open, basically Mammoth Hot Springs and the Lamar Valley.

I wanted to get as much done as possible before the snows hit, as I'm not much for winter, then I would go home for the rest of the year, work on production, and return in the spring.

But what happened instead was that I fell in love with Yellowstone and didn't want to leave. I made a few friends there in Gardiner, as I would go hang out at the headquarters of the Yellowstone Foundation, now called Yellowstone Forever, the nonprofit partner of the national park. They were very supportive of my project and even wanted to sell my album in their store when I finished it.

I loved the little town of Gardiner, especially in the off-season, and the fact that the Yellowstone River ran right through the middle of it was just icing on the cake, as it allowed me to make some nice recordings from right in front of my cabin.

Gardiner isn't far from Mammoth Hot Springs, so I also went there and got some great recordings of the hot springs bubbling, as well as of the many elk that basically live on the grounds there.

But what I really liked was the Boiling River, there at the north end of the park between Gardiner and Mammoth. A nearby sign marks the 45th parallel of latitude, an imaginary line that circles the globe halfway between the equator and the North Pole.

The Boiling River isn't really a river at all, but a stretch created where the Boiling River Hot Spring mixes with the cold water in the Gardner River. It's like a natural hot tub, a great place to soak up the natural beauty of Yellowstone.

Just as an aside, the Gardner River was named for a fur trapper in the 1830s, and the town of Gardiner was later also named for him, but they spelled it wrong, so you now have two different spellings. The Gardner River empties into the Yellowstone River near Gardiner. Kind of confusing.

So, I got to soak in hot water, exactly midway between the equator and North Pole, while doing some recording. It's one of the few places in the park where they allow you to get in the water. I'll never forget sitting there thinking I had the greatest job in the world.

Anyway, I guess I'm a creature of comfort, as I would often go to the Boiling River and soak, reveling in the fact that I usually had it all to myself, knowing it was a crowded place in the summer.

The town of Gardiner is much more than a tourist town, for it seems like a lot of the people there are real hard-core Yellowstone lovers, a number who are retired from park employment. In fact, that's where I met the man who would become my husband, Dan.

Now, I'm not a kid anymore, and I certainly wasn't looking for a partner, having been divorced, but Dan and I hit it off from day one. There was just something about the two of us together—it wasn't particularly romantic as much as we just had a lot of fun and enjoyed the same things.

We became good friends, then later decided to get married, which is probably the best way to do things. Dan's wife had passed away a number of years ago, so we were both single.

Dan was a retired ranger and a walking encyclopedia when it came to the park, and he knew some really interesting stories, things that weren't in the books. I will add that what happened later, right there at Boiling Springs, wasn't entirely a surprise to him—well, in theory, anyway—as he'd heard all about it, even if it was all second-hand to him until then.

It seems a number of people who know the park are aware of things going on but don't want to scare the tourists.

Well, Dan and I started hanging out together more and more, and before I knew it, winter had come and my plans to go back home to Las Vegas were pretty much forgotten. I spent a lot of time at Dan's house, a small place on the edge of town with great views of the mountains.

Now, even though Dan and I were both in our late 50s when all this happened, we were in great shape, and once the snows hit, we loved to go cross-country skiing.

After we were done, we'd go the three miles or so from town to the Boiling River and soak. The park technically closes the river after dark, but there's never anyone there to enforce it in the winter.

So, we'd occasionally find ourselves still in the water, watching the sunset and drinking a glass of wine after a long day of skiing, not getting out until well after dark. It was paradise—well, until one day, anyway, which I'll get to soon.

One morning, Dan and I were sitting in his kitchen drinking coffee while he helped me make a list of things to record when I came back next spring.

"You can do loons, meadow larks, bison in rut, frogs, ravens, fumaroles, mud pots, magpies, Puff 'n Stuff Geyser, and Dragon's Mouth Spring," he said, getting excited.

"Dragon's Mouth Spring sounds cool," I replied.

"It's a steam vent that makes weird sounds. And there's Black Sand Pool, where the ground shakes from the low-frequency thumps made by bubbles deep down in the spring."

He paused, thinking, then added, "But I have an idea, why not add something different and do some night sounds? In the summer, there are lots of insects and birds that come out at night. And winter's a good time to record coyote and wolf howls, as they hang around the valleys looking for lunch, since that's where all the buffalo and elk stay."

I thought it was a great idea. We could go out to the Lamar Valley at night and maybe record wolves and coyotes singing.

We decided to go the very next day, as the weather was good. We'd pack a picnic and head out in the late afternoon. Since it was only about a 45-minute drive to the heart of the valley, we'd get there in time to watch the buffalo herds and maybe get some sunset photos.

It was a beautiful evening, and even though we never did hear any wolves, I did manage to get a good recording of coyotes yipping. They were actually very close, almost as if they knew what we were doing and wanted to cooperate.

It wasn't that late when we reached Mammoth, so we decided to stop and soak in the Boiling River. We each carried a good flashlight, so the half-mile walk from the parking area by the highway was easy to find, though I admit it was a bit spooky getting into the river, as you couldn't see anything but steam.

We sat there, very quiet, listening to the gurgling of the water, kind of half-spooked, though Dan said he felt fine. Maybe it was my intuition, but I didn't feel fine, and I told him I didn't want to stay long.

He seemed disappointed, wanting to soak longer, but after about fifteen minutes, we got out.

On the way back, we talked about how I'd felt, and we both pretty much chalked it up to me not liking being in the river in the dark, even though it wasn't at all deep that time of year.

Well, Dan told me he'd been going to the Boiling River for years, both alone and with friends, though he would never go alone at night. I asked if he'd ever felt weirded out, and he said only one time, when he'd heard something in the brush nearby.

He was with a friend and they'd hightailed it out of there. Even though it was winter, they'd thought it was a bear. I didn't know this, but he said sometimes bears will wake up in the winter and leave the den for awhile, then go back in and hibernate.

Well, I was determined to get some good recordings of wolf howls, so the next day we went back to the Lamar Valley. There's a whole network of people in Gardiner who are wolf watchers. Some of these people are professional wildlife photographers.

The park used to give out the locations of the wolves by tracking their radio collar signals, but they don't provide that information anymore, as it was getting to be too invasive for the wolves with people trying to follow them.

Dan knew everyone in Gardiner, of course, and once they found out what we were doing, his friends would call him anytime the wolves were sighted near the highway. We got to where we went to the Lamar Valley at least twice a week, sometimes daily.

And in spite of my earlier trepidations, we would almost always stop at the Boiling River on our way back, usually in the dark. It was just so relaxing—physically, at least—though I will admit I was still on edge mentally, though I did start to mellow out some. But I did start bringing a can of bear spray with my swimsuit and towel, though I didn't tell Dan.

Yellowstone has an incredible history, all the way back to the Native Americans and early explorers and trappers. It also has an incredible geological story, but what's really interesting and often not told are the more mysterious tales of the park. Dan knew them all, from the archaeology to the stories of spooks haunting Old Faithful Inn.

For some reason—and I didn't really think about it much until later—he started telling me odd stories every time we went to the Boiling River. I don't think he was trying to scare me, I think it was just that the setting was so appropriate, with the swirling mists and mysterious sounds of the water.

Most of his tales were pretty unbelievable, like the story of the gold prospectors in the 1870s who had their horses stolen by Native Americans. Supposedly, the natives got swept over the lower Yellowstone Falls with the stolen horses. Sometimes people supposedly hear chanting there and the water turns red.

Dan loved geology, so he would talk about things like the underwater geysers in Yellowstone Lake. And since much of the park is an active volcano's caldera, there are lots of interesting things everywhere.

But he always came back to this one thing that truly puzzled him. He and other rangers had heard strange calls and sounds that nobody could identify, sounds that always left the listener shivering in their boots. And of all the strange things Dan would talk about, this was the one that always gave me the creeps and would make me want to leave the Boiling River.

Of course, he was talking about Bigfoot, but he would never call it that, as he felt it lessened it and made it seem like a silly myth, something with big feet and a big ugly face. He would always call them hominid-like creatures, ones with enough intelligence to avoid humans.

He had a theory, and apparently it was shared by some of his fellow rangers, that this was a real animal that had long ago found the park as a refuge from human encroachment. Given that most of the park is never visited by humans, it would indeed be a good place to hide out.

When I would ask him if he'd ever seen one, he'd say no, but he'd seen evidence of them in the form of footprints, and had heard them many times when he was in the backcountry.

It would always give me the chills, ironically, sitting there in the hot water. But when I would ask if they were dangerous, he would say he didn't think so, though I got the feeling he wasn't entirely convinced.

Well, it was now mid-January, and the park was locked in deep ice and snow. I'd finally been able to make some really good recordings of wolves howling, and I felt it was time for me to go home to my studio, as well as to get away from the cold. I hated to leave, but I was anxious to get this part of my Yellowstone album done so I could come back in the spring.

So, Dan and I decided to spend my last evening there at our favorite spot in the Boiling River. We took a nice bottle of wine and our swim stuff, and were soon parked there by the highway, ready for the half-mile hike to the river. Since it was dark and there was no one around, I decided to set up my recorder and microphones on the hood of the car. Maybe I could catch some nice night sounds while we were down at the river.

It was a beautiful sunset, and I was starting to feel a little poignant, wondering if I really should just stay after all.

Soon, Dan had started on yet another one of his stories, but this one had a purpose—he was trying to talk me into staying.

"Katie, if you stay, we can take a snowcoach down to Yellowstone Lake and hang out and you can record the Yellowstone Hum."

I told him I had no idea what he was talking about, and he continued.

"The first person to get a recording of this will be famous. Lots of people have heard it, even the 1872 Hayden Expedition. It's been the subject of numerous scientific studies, and yet it's never been explained. We call it *lake music*. It's a strange buzzing sound that moves across the lake."

I was intrigued, wondering why he'd never mentioned it before. Maybe I should stay after all.

He continued. "In 1933, Ranger Watson, caretaker at the Lake Museum, heard the sound nearly every morning for a month. Lots of people have heard it, even a number of geologists, but nobody's ever recorded it. Some people think it's related to the volcanic activity under the lake, or maybe even static electricity."

"Have you heard it?" I asked, the mists swirling around us. It was now dark, and I was beginning to feel uneasy, like we should go.

"I heard it only once in all my years in the park," he replied. "It reminded me of the sound of overhead electrical wires, except it started in the distance and moved overhead like a flock of birds, then faded in the opposite direction. It was really strange. Katie, if you could only record it."

It's hard to describe, but I felt as if I was right there with Dan, experiencing what he'd felt as he told me about the electricity passing over him, so much so that I could feel the hair on my neck standing up.

It took a second for me to realize that I wasn't reacting to his story, but there really was electricity or something around us, right there at the Boiling River, not at Yellowstone Lake.

Dan was suddenly quiet. I could now see his hair was standing on end, as he put his hand on my arm as if to reassure me or even say something. His touching me gave me a shock, then he simply tumbled over, completely passed out in the water.

I instinctively grabbed his arm and began pulling him up and out onto the riverbank, no easy task, for he was totally limp. I finally had him by the shoulders and pulled him out. I was thankful he wasn't a heavy guy.

My first thought was that he'd had a heart attack, as I couldn't feel his pulse. I began CPR, and after a few minutes, was happy to find he had a pulse again. Each time I touched him, I'd get a slight shock, kind of like the static electricity you build up when walking across a carpet or when taking clothes from a dryer.

So far I'd been cool as a cucumber, but when I saw something standing in the shadows of a small stand of trees just across the river, I panicked. The Gardner River wasn't more than 30 feet across and could be easily crossed at that time of year.

Whatever it was, I knew it wasn't there to help and had something to do with Dan passing out. I had to get him to the car, but I couldn't drag him that far, especially over the rocks and uneven path.

Even though I was somewhat panicked, I still had the presence of mind to quickly walk over to the rock where my towel and swim bag were and pull out my bear spray. I then slipped on my shoes, for I knew I was going to have to somehow carry or drag Dan to the car.

But now I was totally panicked. Where were the car keys? Dan's towel and clothes were only a few feet from mine, but whatever was in the trees still stood there, watching, and I was afraid to move. I could see a faint yellow reflection in its eyes, which were a good five feet off the ground.

I finally reached over and grabbed Dan's pants from a nearby rock, finding his keys on a carabiner clipped to a belt loop, then picked up his boots and was quickly back by his side.

The electricity seemed to be gone, and when I touched him again, I didn't get shocked. I felt his pulse, then heard him moan.

"Dan, get up," I whispered. "We have to get to the car." I slipped his boots onto his feet as I said this, still eyeing whatever was in the trees, which hadn't moved.

I pulled him up, and he was able to stand, though wobbly, and we began slowly making our way along the river. I knew that the hike back was going to seem like forever, assuming we even made it.

We stumbled along, me half dragging Dan, until I heard a loud crashing sound behind us. As I turned to look, I could see a dark form splashing across the river, running hard, headed straight for us. I pulled Dan to the side of the trail, then pulled the safety off my bear-spray canister.

It was a moose! A really big bull moose, and as he got closer, I could see sparks flying off his feet as he ran across the rocks, which seemed really odd. Later, talking to Dan, we both decided it must've had some kind of electrical charge, like Dan did.

The moose was soon past us, running as hard as it could, followed by a strange silence and sense of foreboding.

I could now see strange balls of blue electricity rolling down the steep hillside behind the trees. Soon, something entered the small stand of trees across the river, something that shimmered an electrical blue and wavered back and forth in the darkness.

Dan seemed to be getting his strength back and was now moving faster, knowing we had to get to the car. Something very strange and surreal was going on.

I looked back, and now the entire stand of trees was glowing a bluish white, the figure still standing there. Now, from across the valley and behind us, there was a sound like someone yelling "Wooo" in the distance, a prolonged drawn-out call.

Now the figure in the trees started across the river, the water all around it taking on a weird bluish-white cast.

We were soon at the car, where I unlocked it and pushed Dan inside the passenger door, then ran around and jumped in the driver's side, immediately locking the doors.

We'd made it! But to my chagrin, when I turned the key, nothing happened. The engine wouldn't start, and all I heard was the sound of the ignition clicking. I tried again and again, but soon stopped, afraid I would drain the battery.

This was my worst nightmare come true! Dan and I, still in our swimsuits and dripping wet, would quickly freeze to death if we couldn't get the car started, and no one would find us until morning. We were both already starting to shiver.

It wasn't but a minute later that I could see the apparition coming our way, still surrounded by the glowing bluish aura, now having crossed the river. Dan and I both slouched down into our seats as far as we could.

As it approached, I could both hear and feel a strange electrical buzzing at the same time, and when I knew it was next to the car, the feeling was so intense it made my skin itch.

The car's interior was now so bright I could see Dan as easily as if a floodlight were pointed at us. He had his head down, but I made the mistake of looking up.

There, looking in at us, was the strangest face I've ever seen, thick and square-jawed, with eyes that drilled right through me. It was so big it had to crouch over to look inside, and what stood out most was that it had long hair all over its body, hair that was standing straight on end from what looked like an electrical charge.

It seemed to stand there forever, but it was probably only a few seconds, then it left, the glow subsiding until it was dark again.

I was running on autopilot, unable to believe what was happening, but I managed to have enough sense to again try to start the car. Now, amazingly, it started right up.

I was about to take off when I realized my recording equipment was still on the hood, so I quickly jumped out and grabbed it. Driving back to Gardiner, I was terrified that I would see the thing along the highway.

Back at Dan's, we both took long hot showers to warm up, then I borrowed a shirt and some sweat pants, since my clothes were still on a rock back by the river.

I decided to spend the night there, partly because I didn't want to be alone, but also because I wanted to be sure he was OK, even though he said he was feeling fine.

It was a long night for me, though Dan seemed to sleep well. I paced the floor, trying to process what I'd seen.

The next morning, Dan seemed to be low energy, wanting to rest most of the day. We did get a couple of our friends to take us back to the Boiling River to get our clothes, though neither of us really wanted to go.

Back at the river, I began to feel nauseated. Dan didn't want to leave me alone, so his two friends went and got our clothes. Both remarked that the place had an odd odor, smelling faintly like singed grass.

It was a tough decision, but I finally left Gardiner, Dan deciding to go with me. We'd both been unable to sleep, and I kept thinking I saw something looking in the windows, and my appetite was totally gone. We needed to retreat to the sanity and security of a different place.

It was the right thing to do, for once back in Las Vegas, we both seemed to feel better. I soon made good progress on the Yellowstone sound album, and was starting to look forward to finishing it.

We reluctantly returned to Gardiner in the spring and finished up the project, making more recordings around Yellowstone Lake and at the geysers and places we'd been unable to get to during the winter. But I never felt comfortable, and I always made Dan go out with me.

Dan eventually sold his house and moved to his hometown of Thermopolis, Wyoming, where his mom and two grown kids lived. We finally got married, and I joined him there.

And just like when we were in Gardiner, we would often spend our evenings in the hot pools there, though the hot springs in Thermopolis are next to town and feel safe since it's a state park.

We weren't all that far from Yellowstone's eastern gate at Cody, and we figured we would go visit the park once in awhile, but we never did. It was as if we'd lost interest and felt uncomfortable there.

To this day neither of us has a satisfactory explanation for what happened that night at the Boiling River, but Dan really thinks it had something to do with electromagnetism and the volcanic nature of Yellowstone.

I know that sounds really vague, but they say the molten magma in the Yellowstone caldera is only a couple of miles below the surface, and molten magma contains iron. I at first thought maybe it had something to do with this, but then I read that molten iron loses its magnetic properties, so now I have no idea.

Maybe that particular location at the Boiling River has something going on I just don't understand, but since Dan and I had been there so many times without anything happening, I can't help but think it had something to do with the creature itself.

It is possible that the car not starting was just a coincidence, but Dan takes immaculate care of his vehicles, and it started right up after the creature left. Did the creature somehow interfere with the car's electrical system?

And why did Dan pass out, and why did the moose seem to have sparks at its feet? And what about the balls of lightning coming down the slope and the weird glow in the trees, as well as of the creature itself and its hair standing on end?

When I finally got around to checking out my recording, I was shocked, to say the least. The distant yell before the creature crossed the river came through loud and clear. After that, you could hear me and Dan's muffled talking as we made it to the car, then the ignition clicking, and finally, after a few minutes, the sound of static. I figure this was when the creature was looking in our window.

As the static slowly fades, a strange electrical-sounding voice can be heard, but then it morphs into a higher voice saying, "Order more tacos."

I didn't know whether to laugh or cry. The static had apparently made my recorder loop back onto a recording I'd made when Dan and I were goofing off at a local Mexican restaurant. I was showing him how the recorder worked, and I thought I'd later erased it.

I still have the sound of the weird call, but I would give anything to know what that creature had said, assuming I could have understood it.

But I guess it will remain a mystery, just like so many other things in Yellowstone.

5

THE BIGFOOT TAXI

Art came out and spent three days on one of my guided trips on the Yellow-stone River. I really took a liking to him, as he reminded me of my uncle, who'd been a road-grader operator in northwest Colorado when I was a kid.

Art told me he'd wanted to come back to the area for a number of years but hadn't really felt comfortable being very close to the park. He said he'd finally decided to try to overcome his fears, so had come back out, but wanted to be around people, plus he'd always wanted to take up fly-fishing.

He told this story around the campfire to good reception, which was followed by several of the guys wanting Art to go with them into the park and show them around. Art was hesitant at first, but he later contacted me and said he'd spent several days with them at his old haunts and had even had the courage to camp at Madison Campground.

He was laughing as he said it, for all the front-country campgrounds at Yellowstone are usually wall-to-wall people. But he reported that he still felt uncomfortable by Indian Pond, which this story will explain. —Rusty

. . .

Rusty, this is something that I just find completely unbelievable, so I don't expect you or anyone else to think it's true, though it is. This happened years ago, when I was a fairly young guy, and yet it seems like it happened yesterday, it's so clear in my mind's eye.

It all started with me deciding I wanted a different job. I was tired of being a bulldozer operator for a road contractor, primarily because it required I be on the road almost all of the time. I got really tired of living in motel rooms, and I wanted a job where I could go home every evening after work.

I had a friend named Joel who'd worked at Yellowstone for a few years doing their road maintenance, and he said he really enjoyed it, it paid OK, and, best of all, he got to go home every night to a nice cabin there in the park, which was part of the job benefits.

Joel's wife lived there and worked in the park during the summer in one of the stores, and she really liked having the winters off, holing up and making quilts and baking and enjoying the peace and quiet.

Joel thought the work would be something right up my alley, since I'm kind of a loner, though I guess these days they call it being an introvert.

So, I applied for a job with the park, and it wasn't long before I got an offer working as a snow groomer for the coming winter. I would have a cabin at Lake Village, which is on the north shore of Yellowstone Lake. My main job would be running a snow groomer, packing the roads so snowmobilers could use them, which is a pretty big deal in the winter there, as lots of people go to Yellowstone to snowmobile.

I was excited, to say the least. First of all, winter work was hard to come by in the construction business, and I was wondering how I was going to make it financially, as I'd had some unusual expenses like my truck breaking down. My company typically would lay everyone off in the fall and rehire us in the spring.

And best of all, if I did good work and the Yellowstone folks liked me, the odds were good they'd have a permanent position for me in the spring, helping plow the roads for opening day and then maintaining them in the summer.

I realized later that, even though I was definitely qualified for the job, the main reason I got it was because the park had trouble finding people with experience who were willing to spend their winter cut off from civilization.

But it would end up being the only winter I worked there, for numerous reasons—too cold, too much snow, and too isolated. But the real reason, the one that made all the others seemed trivial, is what this story's all about.

As you probably know, Yellowstone has five different entrances, and getting from one side of the park to the other in any direction, east-west or north-south, takes many hours of driving.

It's a huge park, and a lot of people come to visit having no idea how vast it is. I mean, the park has several villages inside it where people typically have to stop and buy gas if they want to make it to the nearest outside town.

But come early November, the park shuts down all the roads except the state highway that runs across the north section, going from Gardiner to Cooke City. After that, the only way you can get into the park is what they call oversnow travel, meaning snowmobiles, snowcoaches, skis, or snowshoes. The roads aren't opened again until mid-April, and some not even until early or mid-May.

Well, I got notice I had the job in mid-November, which meant I had literally a week or two to get everything ready and move to Lake Village. I had to give notice on my apartment back in Michigan, store the little bit of stuff I had, say goodbye to my parents and friends, drive out to Cody, Wyoming, then on in to Yellowstone through the East Entrance. I would then go over Sylvan Pass and on to Lake Lodge by snowmobile, carrying my groceries and stuff on a pull-behind sled.

The thought of it all made me tired, and I almost opted to just stay home. My parents had already told me I could live in their guest cabin through the winter, as they had 20 acres on a lake that was really nice.

I don't know, maybe I should've done that. It's easy to look back at your life choices and wonder if you did the right thing or not, and for every day I spent in that most beautiful of national parks, I probably have had equally as many nightmares, though they are gradually going away.

Well, I hurried as best I could to get out there, but by the time I arrived, sure enough, the roads were closed. There are times when you can still drive in with a ranger if you work there, but it was just my luck that this particular winter ended up setting record snowfalls, and when I got there, the road was passable only by snowmobile.

To make things worse, I was pretty much on my own, as everyone else working there for the winter was already at Lake Village. Back then, the park didn't provide snowmobiles, though they do now.

Fortunately for me, I was able to buy a used snowmobile and sled from a guy in Cody, Wyoming, then I hauled it to Pahaska Teepee, Buffalo Bill's old resort, which was near the East Entrance. There, I made arrangements to leave my truck for the winter.

Well, there I was on my snowmobile, pulling a sled packed to the gills with my supplies, sitting at the closed and locked East Entrance of Yellowstone National Park.

Someone had forgotten to mention I might just need the combination. Back then there was a single gate—today there's a multi-gated entrance.

Because it was just one gate and there was plenty of snow, I was able to just drive around, going through a meadow and dodging trees.

I found out later that there was a ranger stationed there, but he was inside the restaurant at Pahaska Teepee, two miles on down the road, having lunch.

I apparently was supposed to find him at the Pahaska Teepee cafe once I arrived, but nobody told me that. He was going to unlock the gate and accompany me to Lake Village.

So, basically, my first job in Yellowstone was to break into the park. Luckily for me, being from Michigan, I knew plenty about driving a snowmobile, and that knowledge would soon come in handy.

Well, on top of not giving me the combination, nobody told me anything about snowmobiling 30 miles over new snow to reach Lake Village, which would include going over 8530-foot Sylvan Pass, which has 300-foot drop-offs and sits right under aptly named 10,566-foot Avalanche Peak.

If you've ever driven it, there's a sign there that says you're in an avalanche zone, no stopping. You're going through the mighty Absarokas, the mountains that flank the east side of the park.

Well, you've heard people say someone was confident but clueless, but in this case I was confident I was clueless. I decided the route must be pretty easy to find or they wouldn't have left me on my own like that. After all, one of the questions I'd been asked during the phone interview was if I worked well alone and was independent.

After getting around the gate, I will say that the snow wasn't yet deep enough that I couldn't still see the edges of the road, so I wasn't really in any danger of getting lost, as long as I got there before dark.

It was an eerie and yet beautiful drive, as there was no one else around and the only sound was that of my snowmobile. I had arrived between the closing of the gate to vehicular traffic and the opening of the road to snowmobilers. The road was covered with new snow, the only tracks being deer, elk, and moose. I wasn't worried about bears, as they were hibernating.

I'll never forget driving over Sylvan Pass. It was kind of hairy, as the road was narrow and the drop-off intimidating. What was even more intimidating was the knowledge that the route I was snowmobiling would also be the route I would be maintaining with the snow groomer. I would be driving this route often—drop-offs, avalanches, and all.

I had seriously underestimated how long it would take me to get to Lake Village, especially since I was nervous about the pass and took my time. So, when I started down the back side of the pass, dropping towards Yellowstone Lake, I became acutely aware that the sun was starting to set.

I amped it up, soon passing Eleanor Lake and then Sylvan Lake, though I didn't know their names at that time, and eventually reaching the shore of Mary Bay on Yellowstone Lake. The route from there on was more obvious, as it followed the shoreline, but I had to pay close attention, as the lake wasn't frozen. Actually, it's rare for Yellowstone Lake to freeze over, though it has during really cold years.

It was getting dark enough that my snowmobile headlight was all that kept me on the road, and so I slowed my pace.

What happened next should've been a wake up call, but it wasn't until some time later that I realized what was going on.

The road eventually leaves the lake shore and goes through Pelican Valley and right next to a small lake called Indian Pond, which is about one-third of a mile in diameter. I read later that the pond was formed about 3,000 years ago by a hydrothermal explosion, one of the most dangerous and unpredictable events in the park. Superheated water below the surface becomes steam and explodes up through the surface, ejecting boiling water and rocks. In the case of Indian Pond, the crater eventually filled with lake water.

Later, as I spent more time in Yellowstone, I would always have an uneasy feeling when passing Indian Pond and would plow through there as fast as I reasonably could.

But of course, it was my first time there, and by then it was almost dark. My headlamp was bright enough to see where the snow dipped off the roadside, but I was now having to really take it easy, more and more worried about the possibility of getting lost. I strained to see any sign of Fishing Bridge ahead, as I knew I had to cross it before the turnoff to the village.

Just past Indian Pond is a small pull off, then one goes through a small stand of trees, then there's a small parking area that marks the start of Storm Point Trail, a hiking trail leading to a point overlooking Yellowstone Lake. I stopped at that parking area for a moment to get my bearings and clear my goggles.

Now, I didn't know it at the time, but this little stretch of road would become the scene of one of the strangest things that's ever happened to me. But at that point in time, I had no idea of what was out there, or I never would've stopped.

There are people who enjoy reading about mysterious things, but believe me, they're usually in the safety of their own homes. To actually be out there when something weird happens is another thing entirely, especially when it's dark and you're the only one out in a place as wild and as untouched as Yellowstone.

I was afraid to turn my snowmobile off, which is actually something you shouldn't do when out alone like that anyway, in case it won't start, which happens more often than you might think.

So, I was sitting there, at that point pretty cold, my machine running, when I saw something coming up the trail. It had just occurred to me that this was a buffalo and it was acting somewhat aggressive by coming towards me, maybe because my machine was making so much noise.

I decided it was time to continue on, so I quickly stepped on it, my machine lunging forward, making the sled behind kind of snap. Like I said earlier, I had lots of experience on a snowmobile, and I knew how far I could push it without killing the engine or getting stuck, but I wasn't used to pulling a sled.

As my machine lunged forward, so did this buffalo, coming right after me. Man, I was scared, being on the receiving end of a 2,000 pound beast, but when I looked back to see if I was outrunning it, I got even more scared.

Like I said, it was pretty dark, but I could see well enough to know this thing was running on two legs and was no buffalo—and man, it was fast! It had already nearly caught me and was reaching for the back of the sled.

I tore out of there, leaving it in the dust, or I guess I should say snow, afraid at this point to even turn around to look, concentrating solely on not wrecking my snowmobile or dumping the sled.

At this point, the highway goes through the forest for quite a stretch, then opens back up and crosses a short bridge at Pelican Creek. The road was nothing more than a white ribbon through the forest, and I was still high-tailing it out of there, but I had to slow down when I got to the Pelican Creek bridge, as I needed to be careful and not go flying off.

As I slowed down, I could hear the most God-awful sound coming from behind me, maybe a quarter mile away, back near Indian Pond.

Something sounded really angry, and I could hear it whacking on trees and making noises like it was tearing the forest down. This was followed by a mind-bending howl that sounded like a mix of a wolf and a banshee and someone screaming, so loud I could hear it over the sound of my snowmobile. I throttled up and got out of there.

I was soon past the shuttered store and buildings of Fishing Bridge, across Fishing Bridge itself, and then thankfully making the turnoff to the lights of Lake Village.

Once there, I found Joel's cabin, where he and his wife welcomed me, surprised I'd come in alone. I was still pretty shook up about being chased, and as Joel showed me to my cabin and helped me unload my sled, I asked him what it could've been.

Joel was an honest straightforward guy, and he told me they'd been hearing the howls at night since they got there a few weeks before, but figured it was a wolf, though they hadn't been sure, as it sounded so strange and loud.

Well, OK then, I'd made it to Lake Village, where I started my job the very next day. I eventually put that incident behind me, though like I said, I always had a strange feeling when going by Indian Pond. I wasn't sure it was from the memory of that night or for some other reason, but I never liked to stop there, even in broad daylight.

Yellowstone roads typically will get up to 10 feet of snow a year, but my first and only year there was wetter than usual, and it seemed like it snowed practically every day.

And my job was to keep the snowmobilers happy. I typically worked 10 hours a day grooming the roads in the Lake District, keeping them smooth from ruts and snow drifts so the snowmobilers could use them.

My territory went all the way back to the East Entrance, the way I'd come in, and I got to know that road well, including Sylvan Pass, for it was my job to clean the avalanche runoff from the highway there, which at times could be a little harrowing.

Now, you need to know a little about how I accomplished all this in order to understand the rest of this story.

First, I was an experienced heavy equipment operator, and I felt right at home when I first crawled into the cab of the LMC snow groomer I would be driving.

As an aside, I always found it interesting that LMC (the Logan Machine Company, based in Logan, Utah) was originally the Delorian Motor Company (DMC), owned by the same Delorian who made the Delorian car used in the movie, *Back to the Future.*

The LMC groomer was very similar to what you would see on a ski slope. It was a diesel tracked vehicle with a heated cab, equipped in the front with a big dozer blade and in the rear with a drum. It pushed snow ahead of it while the drum packed the snow behind it, smoothing it out for snowmobilers.

A snow groomer goes very slow, under 10 m.p.h., so you have to be a very patient kind of person to drive one, especially day after day. But the more I did it, the more I liked it, and it got to where it was almost a mindless thing for me.

I generally liked the slow pace, enjoying seeing the country and the wildlife, all alone in one of America's most popular national parks. And even though I only lasted that one winter, sometimes I wonder why I didn't keep on and make it my career.

There are lots of worse places to work than for the national parks system. And when things were slow and we didn't get much snow, I could hang around the cabin, doing whatever I wanted.

But back to the snow groomer. You're basically riding along the landscape in a heated comfortable cab, your coffee thermos handy. The visibility was generally good, unless the windows got frosted up, which was a fairly rare thing.

So, pretty much every day, I would get up, go to the shop and gas up my LMC snowcat, then head out, slowly grooming the road as I went. And the days that the snows were bad, I often didn't get back until after dark, though I hated that, as visibility could get pretty bad. And, like I said, I always got the creeps when I drove by Indian Pond.

Sometimes, when I'd get to the East Entrance and the park

ranger, Jim, would be around, we'd go have lunch together at Pahaska Teepee.

One day, I told Jim about how the pond made me feel and asked if he'd ever felt that way. He looked at me for a long time, then said, "It's interesting that you say that, cause I've had the same feeling at Indian Pond and at several other places in the park. It's not like bears or buffalo or anything like that, it's just creepy. The top of Sylvan Pass does that to me, and I have no idea why, but I refuse to stop there. I always thought it was maybe because it's an avalanche zone, but other avalanche zones make me feel unsafe, but not creeped out."

He paused, thinking, then added, "I think there's something out there that we don't understand, Art."

I then told him about the howling, asking, "Do you think that could be a wolf?"

Jim had a degree in wildlife biology and had worked in the park basically his whole life, having got the job right out of school.

He replied, "No. I've heard it before, too, and it's definitely not a wolf."

"What else could it be?"

"Your guess is as good as mine. This park has been protected since its inception in 1872. It was the first national park not just in the U.S., but in the entire world. Things that were hunted out or forced to relocate in other places because of human intrusion were lucky here and didn't face that encroachment."

Jim paused to sip his coffee, and I was beginning to think that was all he was going to say about it when he added, "I've talked to other rangers who say the same thing—there really is something out there. We don't like to talk about it for several reasons: it scares the public, we don't understand it, and we're basically scared to death of it ourselves. There's an unspoken rule among the green and gray that we don't scare the public."

"The green and gray?" I asked.

Jim pointed to his uniform. "Park colors."

"Do you think it's dangerous?" I asked.

He replied, "I don't know, but sometimes it sure sounds like it would like to kill somebody."

"Have a lot of people gone missing in the park?"

Jim replied, "Yellowstone usually has way fewer missing people than the other parks. Most of the missing are in places like Yosemite and Great Smoky Mountains, where there's much higher visitation. Right now, there's nobody unaccounted for here."

It was an interesting conversation, and as I drove back over the pass, I slowed down and made special note of how I felt at the top. Like Jim had said, it felt kind of eerie, but nothing like Indian Pond.

It was dusk when I arrived at Indian Pond, and I again felt like something was wrong there, and I was pretty sure what it was. I again had that same uneasy feeling, one that surely had to do with what I'd seen my first time through there.

I was almost past the pond when I saw that something had really messed up the snowmobile track there. I'd just groomed it earlier that day on my way over to the East Entrance, and now it looked like something had made deep ruts in the road.

As I got closer, I could see that someone had dragged a bunch of branches over the road, the shadows making them look like ruts. The last thing I wanted to do was get out of my machine, but I had no choice, as the limbs were too big to push out of the way. I would have to drag them off the road.

I was scared to death, as I knew what had tried to block the road. As I dragged the branches off, one by one, I had a feeling of heightened awareness, my senses on edge, like I was being watched, and the hair stood up on the back of my neck.

And as I finished, it was then that I saw the tracks leading away from the road. These were not like anything I'd ever seen, but were huge tracks that walked two by two like a human, but much larger and deeper and with a well-defined toe outline.

I jumped back into the cat and got the heck out of there, half expecting to again hear the roaring howl, but all was quiet.

Well, I can tell you that none of this set very well with me, and I had trouble sleeping that night. I kept getting up and peeking out the window, sure I was going to see something.

The next day was quiet without a lot to do, so after some machine maintenance, I found my friend Joel and asked him what he thought.

His reply was pretty succinct—he loaned me his loaded 30.06 Springfield rifle to carry in my cab. Keep in mind that at that time, it was illegal to carry weapons in the park unless you were a law-enforcement ranger. You can now legally carry them as long as they're unloaded.

I put the rifle in a hidden but handy spot in the cab the next day and headed out for the East Entrance again, since it had snowed during the night. Nothing was unusual when driving by Indian Pond, and I could still see the branches I'd pulled off the road the night before, confirming it wasn't my imagination.

Now, like I mentioned before, you're going across Pelican Meadow on this stretch of road, but there's one small stand of trees you pass before you reach the pond. And as I drove through there, something really strange happened—I felt a big thunk on the roof of the cab, like something had fallen onto it.

If it had been any place but Indian Pond, I would've stopped and checked it out, but after the event of the previous night, the last thing I wanted to do was stop.

I kept going, listening closely to hear if anything was amiss. The machine seemed like it was having a bit more trouble than usual plowing snow off, but everything seemed to be working OK.

And since the noise had come from the roof and not the engine or tracks, I finally decided it had to be a large branch that had fallen onto the cab, or worse, been purposely dropped onto the cab.

The new snow was fairly light and dry, so I was making good time heading up the pass, enjoying the scenery, the trees and rocks covered with a beautiful hoarfrost that I knew wouldn't last long in the sun.

Like I said, I would get into a mindless state sometimes, and it didn't seem like it had taken all that long before I was coming to the top of Sylvan Pass. I'd pretty much written off the thunk noise as a branch, figuring it had come off along the way.

I slowed down, partly because I was now going through the avalanche zone and was expecting possible debris, but also because I was thinking about what Jim had said about it feeling spooky up there. I wanted to again see how the place felt, though I sure didn't want to tarry, given the dangers.

Suddenly, something blocked my view, and I instinctively slowed, for something was hanging in front of me from the roof of the cab. If it had been white, I would've known it was snow sliding off the roof, but it was black as night.

I struggled to make out what it was as I stopped, but when I finally could see that the black mass had eyes, I was shocked. There, hanging just a few feet in front of me, the only thing between me and it but windshield glass, was some kind of creature that looked exactly like an ape-man, if there were such a thing.

Its eyes were large and dark green with no apparent iris, and it had broad cheeks and a square jaw. Long scraggly hair hung down everywhere except around its face, which had dark leathery skin.

But what really got to me was how human it looked, and not only did it look human, but it had an expression on its face like you might see on a teenager who'd just played a practical joke on you. For some reason, I knew it was young, and I also knew it was what I'd felt hit the cab at Indian Pond. It seemed like it was gloating about its cleverness at hitching a ride to the top of the pass.

All of a sudden, the face disappeared, and it felt like a weight was lifted from the cat. I glanced in the rear-view mirror just in time to see something dark running up the steep bank by the highway, and if you've ever driven Sylvan Pass, you'll know I mean steep.

Rocks clattered down the bank, and I now pushed the snowcat as fast as I felt safe, as it was the last place I wanted to be if the whole bank slid. As I drove on, I craned my head back and could see the black figure was now topping the huge bank. I was amazed at how fast it had climbed that incredibly steep slope.

I went on down to the bottom of the pass, then stopped and

poured myself a cup of coffee from my thermos, shaking. It hadn't snowed much on that side of the mountain, so I did something I'd never done before—I turned around before finishing the job and went back home.

And as I again topped out, reaching the summit of the pass, I slowed just enough to see the same type of huge tracks I'd seen down by Indian Lake, tracks going almost straight up the slope as if it was flat.

I made good time going home, not even slowing when I reached the edge of Pelican Meadows, where I would often stop and take a break. In fact, I'm pretty sure that was the fastest run I ever made before or since.

That night I could barely sleep, a repeat of my first night there, every little sound outside the cabin turning into what I knew had to be a Bigfoot, as I was pretty sure that was what was going on.

A Bigfoot. I'd always laughed when anyone talked about them, being a practical kind of guy. I didn't think it was impossible for them to exist, but I sure as heck didn't think they were very probable.

But there really was nothing else to explain what I'd seen and heard. And I knew Jim and probably a lot of the other rangers believed in them, though I was sure they would never admit it.

I knew one thing at that point, I didn't want to be in Yellowstone any longer. I'd really enjoyed my time there, the job fit me perfectly, and I liked the thought of having permanent employment, but I dreaded the next day's run.

I got up really early, unable to sleep, thinking about everything. Was my job worth my life? I hadn't worried too much about getting caught in an avalanche, even though I knew at least one snowcat driver had died on Sylvan Pass, but this was something new, something I wasn't sure how to process mentally.

Was the thing gone? I knew I'd given it a taxi ride to a new spot in the park. Maybe it was on an early spring migration to Canada or something. I could only hope.

But the really important thing here was that it hadn't tried to harm me. It had apparently ridden along quietly on top of my cab, then looked inside the cab, maybe even gloating at its cleverness, then jumped off when it got to where it wanted to be. If that was the worst it would do, what was there to worry about?

Well, trying to talk myself out of being scared to death wasn't working very well, but I was a man of my word and I'd hired on until spring, so I would stay, though at that point I was losing any desire for permanent employment there.

The next run, I took the groomer as fast as possible through the Indian Pond area, then again over Sylvan Pass. I saw nothing in either place, which was a relief.

I didn't have lunch with Jim again after that, as I no longer wanted to take a break but to just turn around and get it over with. I did decide to contact him at some point and tell him about everything, but figured it would be better if I did it after I left. I guess I just wasn't ready to talk about it.

I can't tell you how much I looked forward to the end of that seasonal job, and when the park called and asked if I would continue on as a permanent driver, helping plow out the roads for the spring opening, I had to decline.

I'd finally reached my goal of getting stable well-paying employment while doing something I enjoyed, but I couldn't help it, I had to turn it down.

So, it was back to Michigan, where I stayed at my parents' place until I finally got a job working for the county road crew.

It wasn't nearly as beautiful as Yellowstone, but I didn't have to live in a remote area in the winter and hope I didn't get smashed by an avalanche every day.

But all in all, I did miss the park, and some days even wished I was back there.

It was about six months after I left that I gave Ranger Jim a call. For some reason, I felt like we were birds of a feather, and I wanted to stay in touch.

We talked for a bit, and he finally told me he was leaving Yellowstone after 15 years there, transferring to a ranger position at Bryce Canyon, even though it was a step down in terms of a career path.

Yellowstone was more prestigious with more responsibility and therefore higher pay. But he said he didn't care, he just wanted out of there.

This really surprised me, for we'd had lots of good talks over lunch at Pahaska Teepee, and he'd told me he would never leave the park.

I didn't want to pry, but it felt like there was something he wanted to tell me, but was reluctant to do so. I decided it would be a good time to tell him how I'd provided a taxi service to a Bigfoot, though I wondered if he would believe me. But it might help him understand why he always felt the top of the pass was spooky, if it was part of a Bigfoot thoroughfare.

But Jim acted like he believed me completely, which surprised me a little. We then talked a bit more about our future and how I might get to Bryce someday and meet up for lunch.

It had been a pleasant conversation, and I thought he was about ready to say goodbye when he told me he, too, had something he wanted to tell me, but I had to promise to keep a lid on it and not tell anyone at the park.

I agreed, and he added, "Art, you know, what you said just made me understand better what I'm about to tell you."

He paused for the longest time, and when I was thinking he'd changed his mind, he continued. "Not long after you left, I was down at the East Entrance when one of the park's snowplow operators radioed me, asking if I'd come up to the top of the pass. They were plowing out the roads for spring opening."

"What happened?" I asked.

"Well, I really didn't want to go up there, as it was a long ways on a snowmobile, and I asked him if it was really necessary. It was funny, he acted like he didn't want to talk about it on the radio. So, we went back and forth a little, then I agreed to go on up."

He continued. "It took me awhile to get there, but when I did, he said he had something he wanted me to get a good look at. It was something there in front of his blade, something half buried in snow that he'd plowed up from the runoff of an avalanche. So, I walked over there and took a look, and man, it shook me to the bottom of my very core, and I know it did him, too. I only wished I'd brought my camera, but in the long run, I was glad I hadn't. Who wants a picture of something that creepy looking?"

"Was it the same thing I gave a ride to?" I asked.

"It was," Jim replied. "I told him to push it off the side in that place with the 300-foot drop off, and hopefully it would be covered with avalanche rocks and debris before things melted out too much. He did that, and we then parted ways. Neither of us ever mentioned it to each other again, though I saw him almost every day, and I didn't file a report. As far as I know, it's still in that drainage below Sylvan Pass, hopefully deeply buried."

I thanked Jim for telling me, then said goodbye. In the long run, I knew my promise to not tell any one at the park would be easy to keep, because nobody would believe either of us anyway.

6

A HOT WINTER'S BATH

I occasionally get private parties wanting me to guide them for a day or two, and I really enjoy this type of work, for I get to go back to my comfortable bed at night instead of camping, plus I get to know people a little better than when I have a larger group.

I was guiding this couple on the Yampa River in Colorado, having a great time, when I discovered that they used to vacation every winter in Yellowstone. When they found out that I sometimes guided in Montana, we had a great talk about the wildlife there, which eventually led to the following story. —Rusty

Rusty, one of the highlights of my year used to be when my husband Tom and I would vacation in Yellowstone. It had become a tradition with us, and we always went in the winter, specifically in January, for my birthday.

Everyone would always ask, why in the winter? Yellowstone is a very cold place with lots of snow, and it often has subzero temperatures. Winter would seem like the worst time to visit.

All it would take is one trip there, and you would immediately understand. It's absolutely gorgeous in the winter with all the snow, and the geysers create hoarfrost on all the nearby trees and also sometimes even on the buffalo, who tend to hang around there where it's warmer.

You also get to see more wildlife in winter, as they've come down from the mountains to the lower valleys. All the bears are hibernating, which means you can snowshoe or ski wherever you want without worry, as long as you stay away from the moose and buffalo.

I know they're technically bison, but everyone there, even the rangers, calls them buffalo. They're huge animals, and because they hang around the geysers so much, you can often watch them from your room.

I'm referring to the Old Faithful Snow Lodge, which is where we always stay. You can also stay in the Mammoth Hot Springs section of the park, but because you can drive there, you'll see more people.

And that leads me to the real reason we go in the winter—the lack of people. Yellowstone has so many visitors in the summer that it really detracts from the experience, unless you go backpacking, then you have the bears to worry about.

In the winter, you'll see very few people, and most of them will be diehard Yellowstone fans who have made a great effort to be there.

But going in the winter can be expensive, primarily because you have to book a snowcoach to get there and have to stay in the park's lodging, as all the campgrounds are closed—but it's too cold to camp, anyway.

Because you can't drive into the park in the winter, snowcoaches and snowmobiles are the only way you can get there. Mammoth is open to cars because it's so close to the state highway that goes from Gardiner to Cooke City, which they have to keep open. But the rest of the park is closed to vehicles.

Just riding on a snowcoach to the Old Faithful area is well worth the cost. It's so beautiful, gliding through the snowy landscape. They're nothing like snowmobiles, as they can carry a dozen people and you ride in warmth and comfort, plus you're safe from buffalo encounters. Snowcoaches are kind of like a small bus with high clearance and big wheels, though some have tracks.

Anyway, I wanted to tell you all this so you could get a feel for what I'm about to relate. All I can say is that after this event, we decided to never go back to the park again, which is pretty drastic considering how much we loved it there.

It forever changed the park for both me and my husband. We'll never feel comfortable there again, so we quit going. Actually, we don't feel so comfortable out in the woods anymore, no matter where we are, but we find if we stick closer to our home turf of Arizona, we don't feel quite as uneasy.

Okay, so what happened that made us feel this way? It started with a kind of intuitive feeling that something was wrong, then evolved into a deep fear we had the entire time we were there.

We always timed our visits with a full moon, for seeing the geysers lit up at night is a magical experience. And having a full moon did make everything seem more mysterious, but what we saw —well, we saw it in full daylight. There's no question as to what it was.

And later, I thought about all the previous years when we'd gone out on the boardwalk under a full moon to see the geysers, and it gives me the creeps, wondering what might've been watching us. We're probably lucky we didn't have something bad happen to us.

After we left the park, I thought about it a lot. Yellowstone is such a huge place, it makes me wonder what else goes on there that nobody knows about. I'm sure there's plenty.

Anyway, we'd gone there so many times that we had a special room at the Old Faithful Snow Lodge that we always reserved in advance. It was special because it's one of the few rooms where you can see Old Faithful Geyser from the windows. The historic Old Faithful Inn is the best place to watch the geyser, but the inn is closed in the winter.

So, our first day there, after arriving via snowcoach and unpacking our suitcases, I was finally able to relax in our room while Tom went to get a take-out lunch from the lodge's restaurant.

As I sat there, looking out the window, I could see steam floating through the trees, covering everything with hoarfrost, and it finally sank in where I was. I finally began to feel the excitement of being there. I swear, all the hassle of traveling that far consumes you, but once you're there, it's well worth it.

It was early afternoon, and a few people were out on the board-walk that surrounds Old Faithful and goes around the geyser basin. It was kind of interesting watching them, wondering where they were from and how they'd come to be in Yellowstone.

It had just snowed, and though the geyser basin is warmer than most of the park, it can still get a good buildup of snow. And since the boardwalks aren't shoveled, they can sometimes get icy.

I was glad we'd brought our micro-spikes, which would give our boots good grip on snow and ice. A number of people have died from getting off the boardwalk and falling through the thin crust into the hot pools, and we certainly didn't want to worry about sliding around in a place like that.

I could see that Beehive Geyser was going off in the distance—it's not that far from Old Faithful. If you've never been there, the area is pretty much like a large meadow with clumps of trees behind, the forest stretching up the hills behind. You can tell where the geysers and hot pools are from where the clouds of mist are.

This part of the park has the highest concentration of geysers of anywhere in the world, with over 250, most of which are by the Fire-hole River, which isn't far behind Beehive.

Of course, Old Faithful is the most popular of all the geysers, mostly because it erupts about every 90 minutes and puts on such a good display. It's very photogenic and people love it.

The boardwalk circles Old Faithful, then has a section that loops back behind Beehive Geyser and accesses a number of smaller geysers, such as Giantess and Doublet Pool. A loop trail crosses the Firehole River and climbs the hill through the trees to Observation Point and Solitary Geyser, a hike we hoped to do during this visit.

As I waited for Tom in our room, watching the steam rising from the beehive-shaped travertine of Beehive Geyser, something caught my eye, some kind of movement back in the trees.

I was sure I could see dark shapes back in there, and I figured they must be buffalo, as they hang around the geyser basin a lot in the winter where it's warmer.

Whatever the dark shapes were, they were soon gone, and my husband arrived with our lunch. We enjoyed our soup and salad while looking out the window at the misty and serene landscape, talking about what we wanted to do while there, getting more and more excited.

Happy as we were to be there, we were tired, and neither of us wanted to do much more that day. The snowcoach trip and getting settled had been enough. But later, just before dark, we did take a stroll around the boardwalk just in time to see Old Faithful erupt.

Even though we'd seen it many times before, it was always a thrill, especially when you thought about what was causing it, hot water underground shooting up when the pressure got high enough.

Most people, even though they know Yellowstone is volcanic, aren't aware that a good portion of the park, including where we were at that moment, is in the volcano's caldera. Deep under the surface, hot magma heats the rocks where fissures of water lead to the geysers.

It's kind of scary when you think of it, especially the part that it could eventually erupt again, but it's closely monitored, and geologists say a major earthquake there is a bigger concern, at least in our lifetimes.

But we weren't too worried about that, and it felt good to stretch our legs. Even though the boardwalk was icy, we walked all the way around Old Faithful to Beehive Geyser.

Tom wanted to stay out to get a picture of Old Faithful lit up by the sunset, but as we waited, I started to feel uneasy. It was almost as if something malevolent was watching us, but it didn't make sense, because there were no buffalo nearby, and all the bears were in hibernation. What else could it be?

I told Tom I felt we should get back, and he agreed, saying he could feel it also. We barely got back to the lodge before dark, and I kept turning around to see if we were being followed. At one point, I thought I saw the dark shadows back in the trees I'd seen before, but it was too misty to make out much.

After a nice dinner in the lodge's restaurant, we read for awhile, then went to bed early, tired and happy to be in our favorite national park again. It had been a good day, and we'd mostly forgotten the odd feeling we'd had out on the boardwalk.

But our rest was to be short-lived, for something woke us in the middle of the night, something that sounded like scratching against the wall.

I got up and looked out the window to see a buffalo scratching its side against the building. It was soon joined by two more, and they stood there, eyes focused on the geyser basin as if watching something.

From what I could tell from their size, it appeared to be a mother and two youngsters, maybe calves from previous years, as one was almost full-grown and the other a bit smaller.

Tom also got up, and we could've reached out and touched them if the glass hadn't been there, they were so close. It made us realize just how massive they were—there was a reason they weren't afraid of anything—or were they?

What were they watching? They didn't seem agitated, just alert. Maybe there were wolves nearby. Buffalo are very adept at thwarting wolves, and a park ranger had told us once that wolves, on average, have successful hunts only about one out of five times, and usually these are the sick or injured. One way buffalo keep wolves away is by standing together in herds, so why were these three alone if there was danger?

Tom finally went back to bed, saying they were near the building to stay warm. I was ready to join him when I saw the buffalo suddenly turn and bolt around behind the building.

What had scared them? I looked back towards the geyser basin, and it was then that I saw what appeared to be someone walking towards the lodge along the boardwalk.

Who would be out in subzero temperatures in the middle of the night? I decided it had to be someone out photographing Old Faithful erupting against the night sky. That was true dedication, I thought, and as the figure got closer, it looked like someone really big, though maybe they were just bundled up for the cold.

But instead of coming to the lodge, they continued around the boardwalk, fading into the mists. I thought it was odd they didn't come inside the lodge, but I went to bed and thought no more about it.

The next morning, at breakfast, we asked the waitress about the buffalo. She said that they come around the lodge for the warmth, and we should be wary of them, for though they were seldom aggressive, they were unpredictable.

That day, we'd decided to go snowshoeing, and we had the lodge make us sack lunches to take along. Even though we planned to only be out a half day, we carried daypacks with basic survival gear such as lighters and space blankets.

Since we live in Arizona, the only time we ever snowshoed was when we went to Yellowstone, and we liked it because it took little skill and the slow pace gave us time to enjoy the surroundings. We stuck to the main road, as we didn't want to get into deep snow.

It wasn't long until we met another couple who looked to be our age. Sure enough, they were also retired and came to the park in the winter for the same reasons we did, to enjoy a voluntary winter (they were from Florida) and to get away from the crowds.

We really hit it off and were soon jabbering up a storm, talking about places we'd all been, grandkids, hobbies, that sort of thing. You know how we retired folks are, we entertain each other but are probably pretty boring to younger folk.

We were just snowshoeing along, staying on the snow-packed road, when we came upon three buffalo blocking our way. I knew the odds were against it, but it looked like the same trio we'd seen the previous night rubbing against our wall.

It's very common to see animals in the road in the winter, as it's such a harsh time for them that they choose the easiest paths they can find to conserve their energy. Trying to get them to move is considered a form of harassment by the park. Besides, how do you ask a half-ton animal to move?

Actually, a mature bison bull can weigh up to a ton, or 2,000 pounds, while a female can get to 1,200 pounds, and they can run up to 40 m.p.h., so one treads lightly around them, as they're notorious for being cantankerous.

Well, we stopped, of course, and tried to decide what would be the prudent thing to do. The road was wide enough we could probably pass on by them without them paying us much mind, and I'm sure a seasoned ranger or someone used to them would've done just that.

But the longer we stood there, the more we realized how confining our snowshoes were—we couldn't even get over the high road bank to hide behind a tree. And if we tried to pass them and they turned on us, we couldn't even run away.

The more I looked at these animals, the more I realized how easily we could be stomped or gored to death. Even small buffalo are massive animals, quick and accurate with their horns and hooves—and we were in their territory.

I motioned to turn around, and I didn't have to convince anyone that it was time to turn back. I think everyone was scared stiff, just as I was, and my movement kind of broke the tension.

But to our surprise and concern, the buffalo began following us! We at first thought they were going to run over us, but they seemed to want to stay right behind. It was like they wanted to be nearby, and if we sped up, so would they. It was totally unnerving to have these giant wild beasts behind us.

We again began to wonder if there might be wolves around, which put us somewhat on edge, but we never saw nor heard any evidence of such. The buffalo followed us almost all the way to the lodge, stopping at the edge of the parking lot.

We had dinner with our new Florida friends and discussed the buffalo, which were still hanging around by the lodge. It seemed like they wanted to be around people, but it made us cautious about going outside.

I recalled being in a campground in Glacier National Park, I think it was at Bowman Lake, where there were deer everywhere, and I asked a ranger why they were so tame. Were people feeding them?

He said it was because they knew they were safe from predators when around people. Were the buffalo here doing the same? Was it because there was a pack of wolves around? I figured, like the waitress had said, it was only because they wanted to stay warm near the buildings.

It had been a good day, even though the buffalo had shortened our snowshoe adventure. On the other hand, it would make a good story to tell later when we got back home. I didn't know it then, but having buffalo follow us and hang around was nothing compared to what we saw later.

Back in our room, we had to admit that this trip was quite different from previous ones. We talked for awhile, both confessing that we weren't having all that great of a time.

It was hard to explain, but things seemed different. It just wasn't as comfortable or relaxing. The thought of buffalo hanging around all the time made us realize how close to nature we really were, and not necessarily nature's nice side. We both had an unsettled feeling and were on edge.

Yellowstone has a webpage that has a live stream of Old Faithful, and I thought it was fun to watch it on my laptop while we were there, as I could run right out when it started to erupt without having to wait outside.

I had it on, but wasn't paying it much attention, and Tom was eating popcorn, when he grunted and pointed at the laptop screen. Since it was a moonlit night, we could see steam rising from Old Faithful, as well as from the other geysers in the basin. But we could also see what looked like a line of figures slowly shuffling along the boardwalk, again back towards Beehive Geyser.

It was hard to make out much, except the dark figures looked like they were wearing football uniforms with wide shoulders. They looked vaguely human, but not quite. They soon disappeared into the mists.

We turned out the lights and went to bed, shaken and afraid.

That night the buffalo were back, again waking us by bumping against the wall. Looking outside, I could see what seemed to be the same three that had followed us while snowshoeing. It was hard to tell, but the sizes seemed to match.

Buffalo are very intelligent animals and look out for one another, and will even protect calves that aren't theirs. They seem to have a somewhat advanced social and family structure in each herd, and have territories they visit each season, knowing where the food and water will be best at certain times.

People aren't generally high on their list of animals to pal around with, and a number of tourists have been injured or even killed by them.

Given that, why would they hang around us? Could they be intentionally waking us to make sure we were on alert, maybe trying to tell us something? It sure seemed that way, for they weren't rubbing themselves on the wall, but were banging against it with their hooves, as if making sure we were awake.

I opened the window a crack and started talking to the buffalo, even though Tom said I was crazy. I told them in a reassuring voice that everything would be OK. I have no idea why I thought they might understand me, but they did seem to calm down.

But if I hadn't opened the window, I'm sure I would've never heard the howl. It was eerie, though distant, like over by Beehive Geyser, and the buffalo began to act agitated again.

Tom could hear it from where he lay in bed, and it spooked him, too. He got up and came over to the window to listen. He said it had to be a wolf, but I could tell he wasn't entirely convinced.

To me, it sounded nothing like a wolf—not even close. First of all, it was way too loud for how far away it seemed, and second, it sounded more guttural and almost ape-like, and it lasted too long for a wolf.

After a few seconds, it was followed by a noise back behind the lodge that sounded like someone hitting a tree with a big stick, and every time the thing over by the geyser would call out, whatever was hitting the tree would reply with several tree whacks.

The buffalo seemed truly frightened, softly snorting with their ears laid back, and I wondered later if I weren't somehow personi-fying them and projecting what I was feeling onto them. But when they started acting like they wanted to come into the room, I quickly shut the window and curtains.

These animals had to be scared to death, and I thought of the line of figures we'd seen on the Old Faithful webcam. Buffalo were wild, and their only enemies were wolves. It takes a pretty good pack to take down a buffalo, they're so fearsome, and the only way I could see them hanging around humans was if they wanted food or protection, or maybe warmth. There had been a number of times that buffalo had head-butted cars in Yellowstone and caused thousands of dollars in damage. They weren't particularly cuddly.

The buffalo were gone the next morning, and Tom and I noticed that the lodge didn't seem nearly as busy as it had been. Even in the dead of winter, the lodge is fully booked, so this seemed odd to us.

Our friends from Florida were sitting by the fireplace in the lodge's great room, so we joined them. It didn't take long for talk to turn to how odd things seemed to feel.

They had also noticed a lot of people had left, but didn't know why. We finally asked a lodge employee who was walking by, and he stopped and thought about it for a little bit, then said he wasn't sure, but he suspected it was the weather, as a big storm was coming in.

I didn't say anything at the time, but my thoughts went to the possibility of an oncoming earthquake. There was a lot of anecdotal evidence that animals could sense coming earthquakes, and maybe that was what was bothering the buffalo, not wolves. I wondered if it might not be prudent for us to leave like the others were doing.

After lunch, back in our room, Tom and I seriously discussed whether or not we should go. We weren't having that great of a time, especially compared to previous trips, and if a big storm were coming in, it was possible that the snowcoaches could be grounded and we'd be stuck there, especially if visibility became poor.

Finally, as difficult as it was, we decided to leave that late afternoon, even though we'd lose our reservation money. We called the front desk and reserved spots on a snowcoach, then decided to try to enjoy our final afternoon there as much as possible.

We decided to go ahead and hike the loop trail to Observation Point and on around to Solitary Geyser, as it had been one of our goals for that trip. We'd have plenty of time, as we'd already packed our stuff.

We'd seen pictures taken from Observation Point, and if we could time our arrival there with the eruption of Old Faithful, it would be a good show, as the point was up above everything and gave a good perspective of the area.

I could get a nice panoramic shot of Old Faithful, the geyser basin, the Snow Lodge, and Old Faithful Inn. Since part of the hike was on the boardwalk, we could wear our microspikes and not bother with snowshoes.

We bundled up and grabbed our daypacks with water bottles and snacks, then headed out. We'd checked the board that gave the next eruption time for Old Faithful, and if we didn't dally, we could be at Observation Point shortly before it went off.

Since this would be our last afternoon in the park, we wanted to thoroughly enjoy it, ignoring the strangeness we'd felt. We'd both decided that if an earthquake were impending, maybe we'd get lucky and it would wait until we were gone, and if not, well, so be it, we would enjoy our last hours here either way.

Later, I thought back on all this and decided our behavior, our fears and leaving early, was so unlike us that we had to have instinctively felt the presence of the creatures we were soon to see.

We headed out, noting that there were only a couple of others on the boardwalk, but that wasn't unusual, considering it was winter.

During the high season in the summer, the boardwalk is so crowded you can barely get around.

We walked around Old Faithful and to the Firehole River, which is usually ice free because the waters are so warm. After crossing on a small bridge, we followed a narrow path that crossed a wide grassy area, a popular place for buffalo, though we didn't see any. I wondered where the trio from last night were hanging out.

The entire loop to Observation Point and Surprise Geyser is only about a mile and a half and is easy hiking, so even though it was early afternoon, we figured we had plenty of time before catching the snowcoach. In retrospect, we should've just stayed at the lodge.

After crossing the open field, we entered the forest and began the gradual climb. Normally, being in the trees wouldn't have given me any thought, but I suddenly felt closed in and nervous.

I mentioned this to Tom, and he said he felt the same way and that we should hurry and get to the point.

It wasn't far, and the forest soon opened up, overlooking Old Faithful. It's more obvious there that you're in the caldera of a volcano, which was a bit unsettling, especially given my growing fears about an earthquake.

We sat on some rocks and waited for Old Faithful to erupt, both feeling antsy and nervous. The geyser erupted, and we got what we hoped would be good shots, but we didn't even wait for it to end before starting back.

We soon came to the fork that led to Solitary Geyser, but to be honest, neither of us was very enthusiastic about going. We both just wanted to get back to the lodge. But since we were so close, we decided to go see it anyway, as we had plenty of time.

Thinking about this later, if we hadn't gone to the geyser, we would've missed seeing one of the strangest things ever—actually, *the* strangest thing ever—and missing it would've been a good thing.

We would have never known the true reason we were feeling so strange, and we might still be going to Yellowstone every year. I just don't know. And I really do think it was the presence of these creatures around the lodge that was making everyone feel so weird, so uneasy, even without actually seeing them.

It was an easy hike on over to the geyser, probably about one-third of a mile and gradually downhill, but the minute we stepped back into the forest, which was shady and dark, we both became even more nervous. If we'd listened to our intuition, we would've turned around, but at that point, it was a shorter distance to keep going.

We were soon at a beautiful deep turquoise pool surrounded by orange and red travertine. It reminded me a bit of Morning Glory Pool, probably the prettiest and most photographed object in the park, besides Old Faithful.

Solitary Geyser erupts about every 10 minutes but doesn't get very high, just a few feet. In an area with hundreds of geysers, it gets its name from sitting all alone above the rest.

The geyser had strange yellow wildflowers growing near it called monkey flowers. It seemed odd to see flowers in the dead of winter, but they're able to survive because of the heat from the springs. You can see them there in the summer, too. I took some photos, then we were ready to head back.

We could now see that the trail quickly dropped back to the valley floor, and since we'd gotten out of the trees, we felt a little less anxious, but we were both ready to get back.

But as we started down the trail, we both heard a strange noise that sounded like it was coming from down below near Aurum Geyser, where the trail meets the boardwalk.

It at first sounded like several buffalo fighting, with loud squeals and grunts—but soon turned into an angry howling, and we knew it was no buffalo. It was the exact same type of sound we'd heard our first night there in the room with the window open.

I've never been so scared in all my life, and I could tell Tom was beside himself, for the sounds were coming from right where we had to go to get back to the lodge. And given how dangerous it was to go off-trail, we had no choice but to go that way.

Since the trail wound through thick trees for a bit, we decided to slowly make our way down and hope things had cleared out when we got there, mindful that we had to catch the snowcoach before long. I can't tell you how nervous we both were, walking quietly along, edging our way forward each time the trail turned.

We were almost at the bottom of the hill when Tom held out his hand, stopping me and signaling me to be quiet. There, through the trees, we could see the edge of the geyser basin, and near one of the hot pools we could make out dark figures in the mist. We both froze in terror, then stepped quietly back into the trees.

We couldn't see much because of the steam and mist, but we now heard a moaning sound, higher-pitched than the other howls and growls had been.

Tom turned to me and shrugged his shoulders, as if not knowing what to do, and I'll never forget the look of sheer disbelief on his face. I'm sure mine had the same look.

"Maybe we can make our way around the edge of the trees, staying hidden," I whispered. "Surely the crust is OK where the trees are growing."

"OK," Tom replied. "That's where the buffalo walk around."

I led us though the edge of the forest, which was rough going with downed branches and undergrowth. We slowly made our way around the edge of the geyser basin until we were almost directly across from the dark figures.

We had to cross a small open area in order to continue, and we quickly ran across, terrified that whatever it was would surely see us.

But the figures paid us no mind, and we were soon back in the trees, where we paused to watch in disbelief as the commotion continued. We could now see what was going on.

It appeared that a group of five or six of what I'll call Bigfoot, for a lack of a better term, were holding a smaller one captive. This smaller one was the one doing the moaning, and I later told Tom it sounded young and scared, and he agreed.

The big ones were all dark brown, but the small one was a dirty white. And I call them Bigfoot because they all looked like a combination of apes and humans.

By this, I mean to say they were much larger than a human and very muscular with long arms and thick draping fur, but their faces looked very human, with somewhat flat noses. We weren't close enough to see in detail, but their jaws were square and they looked very powerful.

The white one, definitely a youngster, looked very much the same as the others except it had more of a snout than a nose. It sounded like it was begging for its life, and after it would moan and do what sounded like garbled pleading, the others would start howling and making noises as if they were arguing.

We stood there in shock, forgetting our mission of trying to get back to the lodge. It was almost as if we'd been hypnotized, and I have no idea how long we stood there.

Now, two of the bigger creatures started actually fighting, slamming against and biting each other, but a third quickly broke it up. I had no idea what was going on, but it seemed to revolve around the younger white creature. Were they arguing over what to do with it? It was definitely not a peaceful gathering.

Suddenly, the two Bigfoot who held the white one dragged it to a nearby hot pool and began swinging it, as if they were going to toss it in. It would be a horrible way to die, I thought, gritting my teeth, forgetting our own potential danger.

Just as it looked like the white one would soon be history, another Bigfoot interfered, jumping onto them and making them drop it.

Now, as I held my breath, the white one quickly jumped aside and took off running as fast as it could up the trail we'd just been on. It was lithe and fast, and as the two others started chasing it, I knew they didn't have a chance. They would never catch it.

As they all took off running up the path, Tom and I both came to our senses. We jumped onto the boardwalk, running as fast as we could, thankful for our microspikes on the ice.

We never looked back—we were afraid to! And as we got near the lodge, we could hear the most intense howl, a combination of anger and frustration, and we guessed the white one had escaped, as the sound sounded like it was coming from far up the hillside.

We were quickly in our room, grabbing our stuff, as we had a mere ten minutes before the snowcoach was to leave. It felt like we'd been in a time-warp, for it had been over two hours since we'd been at Surprise Geyser.

Where had the two hours gone? It only takes about 10 minutes to hike from the geyser back to Old Faithful.

We were soon on our way out of the park. We'd come in via West Yellowstone and were going out via Gardiner, as that was the only snowcoach still operating that late in the afternoon, but we didn't care. We just wanted out of there.

We got a room in Gardiner for the night, then arranged for a ride to West Yellowstone the next day via Bozeman.

There, we got our rental car, and after a long drive fighting the incoming storm and bad roads across Island Park, we arrived back at the Idaho Falls airport and flew home.

Interestingly, we never once talked about this incident until several weeks after we'd been back. I think it just took that long for us to regain our sense of well-being and normalcy and to process it all.

When we did discuss it, we had many questions, and Tom's main one was, why did they want to kill the white creature?

He thought it might be because it was different—white with a longer snout, maybe even a subspecies of Bigfoot.

For me, my main question was, did it actually escape? I hoped so.

And we both had to ask how common Bigfoot really were in Yellowstone. Had what we seen been an anomaly, or were they common there?

And why had so many people left the lodge early? Was it from the storm coming in, or did others feel the same unrest and discomfort we did?

We knew we could never answer these questions, and after some time, we began to try to forget what we'd seen.

Did we talk about it to others? No, and our friendship with the couple from Florida suffered because of this experience—we didn't want to be around anything or anyone that would remind us of Yellowstone.

It's actually a shame, for what we once treasured is now pretty much taken away, even if it is by our own desire to forget what happened. We've talked about going back and trying to rekindle our love for the place, but we both admit we'll never feel the same.

Yellowstone will just never feel safe to us again. And I'm sure the millions of visitors who go there every year have no idea of what wildlife is *really* in the park.

7

HIKE YOUR OWN HIKE

I met Zee on the road from West Yellowstone to Bozeman, Montana one late August. He was walking by the highway with his thumb out, and I could tell immediately he was a thru-hiker, as they have a seasoned kind of look after they've been out on the trail a long time.

I stopped and gave him a ride, and once we got to Bozeman, I bought him lunch, then took him to the bus station, as he wanted to get back home to North Dakota.

We didn't talk much after I picked him up, but I could tell he'd had something unsettling happen. Finally, out of the blue, he asked if I believed in Bigfoot, which I found really interesting, considering my hobby is collecting Bigfoot stories. He had no way of knowing that.

I related a few things I thought to be consistent about Bigfoot sightings, and he seemed relieved, though he still didn't say much. I gave him my number as he got on the bus, and to my surprise, he called me the following spring.

I invited him to meet me down on the Gallatin River, where I was teaching some folks how to fly fish for a week. I was actually surprised when he showed up, as he hadn't been sure if he could make it.

After joining us for a few days of fishing, he seemed to relax, and that night, around the campfire, he told us about this remarkable event. —Rusty

. . .

Well, Rusty, I think I may be ready to tell my story. But just as I'm saying this, I feel hesitant and like I should reconsider, as it's not something I thought I would ever relate to anyone. It's just too far out there, kind of like trying to tell someone about a strange dream you had.

You can relate the events and what happened, but you can never really capture the emotions you were feeling during the dream. And sometimes I wonder if it actually wasn't a dream, but it just seems too real.

They say there's a fine line between sanity and madness, and maybe I stepped over that line. I will never know.

I do know that before all this happened, I was leading a pretty normal life, one that was about as good as one could expect, given all the things we have to deal with. Now I feel like I'm sometimes in a fog.

Anyway, I used to be what's called a thru-hiker, and all this happened while I was on the trail. Maybe you're familiar with thru-hiking—it's when you hike some really long trail from beginning to end, though you can do the trail one section at a time.

The Appalachian Trail (AT) is probably the most famous of these kinds of hikes, but there are others, like the Continental Divide Trail (CDT) and the Pacific Crest Trail (PCT). Actually, the three I just mentioned are called the Triple Crown of thru-hiking, but there are other trail.

Thru-hiking has really gotten popular, and social media has helped drive this. There have always been thru-hikers, but the internet now allows people to tell others where they are on any given day, where to find water, the weather on the trail, the conditions, what kind of gear works best, well, you get the picture.

As long as you can occasionally get a wifi connection, you can blog about your trip, put it on Instagram or Facebook or Youtube, and make money from supporters. I think every hiker's dream is to make money while hiking.

Thru-hiking can be dangerous, as you sometimes cross raging rivers, are exposed to the elements, and climb steep ridges and mountains. It's relatively easy to break a leg or an ankle, and there are risks from insects, snakes, and animals.

But in general, it's like hiking anywhere, it's just a lot longer, taking more stamina and dedication. For example, the trail I was hiking when this happened, the CDT, is about 3,100 miles long, going from Mexico to Canada, though my journey ended in Yellowstone National Park.

Now there are, obviously, two directions you can hike a trail, going either north or south, and it all depends on the conditions and which way you prefer.

People going northbound are called NOBOs, and those going south are SOBOs. It's always great to meet people going the opposite direction from you, as they can give you intel on the section you're about to hike.

One other thing, almost nobody that's a thru-hiker uses their real name on the trail. You have a trail name, and it can come from anywhere. By that, I mean you can just decide that's your name, or others can pin it on you, usually because of some incident.

For example, I knew one guy called *Furniture* because he carried a lightweight folding camp chair, which is unheard of with thru-hiking, as the lighter the better. It weighed less than two pounds, but he still got poked fun of for carrying it. And there's a thru-hiker called *Speed Bump* because he'd lay down and rest right on the trail.

My trail name was *Easy* because I was always telling everyone the next stretch of trail was easy. As an ex-military guy, I was in great shape, so a lot of it didn't seem that hard, plus I'm generally an optimist. Over time, the name *Easy* just turned into *Zee*.

So, I was a SOBO on the CBT named Zee. Ha, that sounds kind of funny, but I guess when you're hiking so many miles, you want everything to be short and succinct. Or maybe it's because you're alone so much you forget how to talk, though some people hike in groups.

Not me. The military had been hard on me, and even though I'd been honorably discharged, it had been a miracle, I was so burned out. I was a loner from the git-go, and the military just made me worse.

Oh, and there's a couple of other things about thru-hikes. There are these creatures called *trail angels* who perform *trail magic*. Actually, they're usually other thru-hikers who aren't hiking at the time, or even people who don't hike but want to help out.

Trail angels will go to accessible points on the trail and give thru-hikers food and water, or even take them to the nearest town for a hot shower and meal or to pick up a food drop the hiker mailed to himself.

Trail magic is what it's called when you encounter a trail angel or their work, like a cooler of cold drinks or food that they've left for whoever needs it. A lot of thru-hikers owe their success to trail angels. They're also called *helpers*.

Most people will start at the Mexico border and hike north, because that way they get to the high mountains when it's late summer and the snows aren't as bad. But I'd started at the Canadian border where the beginning of the trail there in Montana was closer to my home in North Dakota. I didn't mind starting later in the season because I wasn't in a hurry. I didn't care if I did it all in one season or two.

By the time I got to Yellowstone, it was late August. I knew at that point there was no way I'd make it through the high mountains of Colorado before the snows hit, so I was taking my time.

I figured I could get through Wyoming's Wind River Range and maybe even into northern Colorado before I'd have to quit. I'd go home for the winter, do odd jobs, then come back where I'd left off. My goal was to enjoy the trail.

I wish now I would've avoided the Yellowstone stretch, like several thru-hikers had advised me. I guess it's some consolation that I wasn't the first to experience what I did, though I didn't know about it until I was actually in the park.

I haven't heard of anyone after me with any strange tales, but that's mostly because I disengaged from the thru-hiker community afterwards, partly because I lost interest and partly because I knew a lot of them thought I was crazy.

How did I know? They told me. It's a tight-knit community, and everyone soon heard about what had happened, especially since I posted on one of the forums about it, warning others off. There was lots of talk after that on social media about Crazy Zee, though a few let me know they were glad I'd been honest, and they were subsequently going to skip Yellowstone.

So, what happened? Well, nothing and yet everything. I swear there's something about Yellowstone that's different, and maybe it's because you're basically hiking through the caldera of an active supervolcano. Why that makes things different I don't know, but I do know things can get strange there.

When you're going south, the CDT enters the Old Faithful region from the Idaho-Montana border, then heads south, missing the mountains. Because you're hiking through a caldera, the trail there is relatively easy, mostly flat with some ups and downs.

There are some stream crossings, and a couple of places that go near hydrothermal stuff where you'd better be careful so you don't break through the crust, but if you follow the trail you're fine. It's for the most part an uneventful fairly easy hike—well, there I go again, it's easy. Except when it's not, which I'll come to in a minute.

It was a really nice day when I reached the park boundary—a crisp cool morning followed by a warm afternoon. I met several NOBOs—all friendly, except one guy who looked kind of stressed, but I figured he was overdoing it or something. He barely said hello.

Now let me mention two hikers I met back when I was about to enter the park. I won't mention them by name, considering everything, but they were two guys probably in their 30s, and both seemed pretty straightforward and honest.

We met before the trail enters the park on the west side, south of the town of West Yellowstone. We talked for a few minutes about things you talk about on the trail, how far you've come, who else is on the trail, that kind of thing, but I could tell they wanted to get going.

They both looked really fatigued, which isn't unusual out on the trail, but these guys could barely talk without looking like they were going to nod off.

I asked them if they were OK, and they told me they'd hiked all night. Now, night hiking isn't that unusual, people will sometimes do it to get back on schedule if they're going to meet someone or that kind of thing, but usually you don't do it.

What was worse was they'd hiked all the previous day and were intending to hike until they basically dropped, which I didn't think would be much longer.

I asked them why they were in such a hurry, and one guy said, "You don't want to know."

I thought that was an odd answer, and I didn't know what to say. Finally, the other guy spoke up and told me they'd had some strange things happen, and they wanted to get as far away from Yellowstone as possible.

I guess they decided that they should warn me, but they didn't go into a lot of detail. They just basically said that they'd been followed by something that they couldn't figure out, because it would never let them see it.

They were pretty sure it wasn't a bear, but they just couldn't make sense of it. It had happened just after they'd left the Old Faithful area, but they were positive it wasn't a person, though they didn't say why. They said it was too weird to explain.

They next encouraged me to consider turning around rather than going on alone. I could hike out with them, and I might want to call it quits like they were as soon as they reached Mack's Inn at Island Park.

I was totally perplexed. I'd met my share of disheartened and burned-out thru-hikers, but I'd never had anyone try to talk me out of continuing. The thru-hiker mantra is "Hike your own hike," and most of them respect that and will leave you to your own devices.

I thanked them, wished them well, then continued towards the park. I felt nervous, but I wasn't sure if it was from what they'd actually told me or if I was just feeling sympathetic to their fears. But like I said, I'm pretty much a loner, and I wasn't ready to quit, yet alone hike out with other people, and I pretty much figured their imaginations had gotten the best of them from fatigue.

So, I continued on towards the park, and it wasn't long until I came to a place in the trail where someone had spelled out YNP in small rocks. This kind of thing is common on these trails, and you'll often see rock markers for milestones, like when you reached every 50 or 100 miles.

I knew YNP was the Yellowstone boundary, and I felt relieved, as I knew I wasn't all that far from the geyser basin and Old Faithful, where I could take a break and resupply.

I was now in the tall forest, and I soon saw red markers on several trees that officially announced I was in Yellowstone, as these had been placed by the park service. And if there'd been any question, I soon came to a yellow sign that some trail angel had placed by the path that read, "CDT Southbound, Welcome to Wyoming."

I was soon crossing miles of deadfall, scars from the big historic fire of 1988. Smaller trees were now taking hold, but there were still thousands of weathered snags and limbs littering the ground. It was slow and tedious, though part of the trail had been cleared.

I could eventually see thermal activity ahead in the form of small plumes of rising steam, and the trail kind of weaved through and around several big hydrothermal pools. I knew it wasn't all that advisable to hike off-trail in this part of the park because of places where the crust was thin and you could fall through.

Well, I can't say I was really enjoying that section of the hike, as deadfall is a pain to navigate, but I wasn't hating life, either. Some stretches of trail you just plug on through, your mind wandering on to other things.

I can't recall what I was thinking about, but it wasn't the trail, as I was on autopilot. But it was about then that I came suddenly back to reality, for the hair on my arms was standing straight up. From nowhere, I felt anxious to the point that I wanted to run.

This was an immediate thing, mind you, not something that built up like the climax of some horror movie. I went from being kind of detached and just hiking along to being in a near panic.

I had the presence of mind to stop and assess the situation, something my military training had drilled into me. I slowly did a 360-degree circle, looking carefully all around, but I saw nothing. And even though I still felt panicked, I forced myself to slowly unhook my bear spray from my belt and take off the safety, then continue on, now thinking of the two hikers I'd met earlier.

OK, what I'm going to describe next may sound impossible, but believe me, it was as real as I am sitting here by this fire right now telling you this story. And it was just the beginning.

I was walking along, past the thermal area and again negotiating deadfall, thinking I would soon be at the geyser basin where there would be lots of people around, when I heard a voice talking to me, but it wasn't like I could hear it with my ears as much as in my mind.

I actually stopped and looked all around, trying to figure out where this voice was coming from, but I finally decided it was my imagination. I wondered how I could be so scared of something from my own mind, then decided I must be getting tired.

This voice in my head was telling me I was going the wrong way, that I should pay attention to the trail because I'd stepped off it and was getting lost. It chided me for being such a poor route finder after all the miles I'd already gone.

Well, I couldn't figure out why I would be lost. It didn't seem like I was lost, and my GPS told me I was fine. I actually got out my compass and map to make sure my GPS wasn't leading me astray, but this also verified I was on trail.

It was weird. I couldn't actually hear this voice, and yet it was as clear as a bell. I looked around, and sure enough, I could now see a trail behind me veering off, and it did look like the main trail. How had I missed it?

But something was wrong, for even though it looked well-used, it was going the wrong direction. I was now totally baffled, but something inside me said to trust myself and continue the way I'd been going, and to hurry like hell and get to the geyser basin.

I suspected I'd run into the same weirdness the two guys had told me about, even though they'd said something was following them, not that they were hearing stuff. And interestingly enough, when I later checked it out on Google Earth, there was no sign of that trail. None at all.

I stepped it up, tightened down my pack straps, and began jogging. I'd learned in the military that one could jog for hours if you took it easy, quickly covering lots of miles. But if you jogged too fast, you'd get a side stitch and have to stop.

Now another really strange thing happened. I'd stopped again for a moment to catch my breath when I heard something coming up behind me on the trail. Just as I turned to see what it was, it went on past me, continuing ahead until it was gone.

It was the strangest thing, like I'd been passed by a ghost, something invisible but with enough weight to make noise as it passed by.

OK, this really freaked me out, but being a pragmatist, I kept trying to figure out an answer, but couldn't come up with anything. I was tempted to turn back and hike out to West Yellowstone, but I decided again it was my imagination.

I started jogging again and finally came to Summit Lake, a small lake that's about halfway between where you enter the park and Old Faithful. I could see that the trail soon entered a much thicker forest, and I knew it followed a drainage all the way to Old Faithful, a good 10 miles or so ahead.

I was tired, having gone a good 15 miles already, part of that jogging. Most hikers stay at Summit Lake, but at this point, I was pretty weirded out, and I wanted nothing more than to be surrounded by civilization and people.

I stopped and drank the rest of my water, also eating a trail bar. I knew I'd have to take the time here to filter more water, as it was the only water source between me and Old Faithful.

It was getting on towards evening, and the thought of night hiking through the trees on a trail that was poorly defined didn't set well, especially considering the weirdness I'd experienced. Maybe it would be better to set up camp, filter some water, and spend the night here, then get to Old Faithful tomorrow.

I was now beginning to have second thoughts about continuing my hike. Nothing said I couldn't quit now and come back in the spring, and the more I thought about it, the more relieved I felt. I was suddenly not enjoying life at all, and that's what I'd gone out there for.

What happened next was one of the strangest nights of my life. I was tired, so after filtering water and having a dinner of freeze-dried stew over my little kerosene stove, I immediately crawled into my bag and went to sleep, even though the place had a strange mysterious feel.

I woke up sometime in the night to a rustling noise. Something was nearby! I always sleep with my bear spray handy, so I grabbed it and my headlamp, slowly opened the tent door, and turned the light in the direction of the sound.

I couldn't believe it! There, not more than 20 feet from me, stood a beautiful gray wolf. I felt a sense of exhilaration, as it was the first I'd ever seen in the wild.

It stood in silence, watching me, then turned and slowly walked away. Not more than 10 minutes later, I could hear what sounded like an entire pack howling in the distance.

I zipped my tent back up, feeling a sense of awe coupled with fear. I knew I was close to the territory of the Mollies pack, and I also knew they posed no danger, but I still felt intimidated, out there all alone. But that feeling was soon replaced by a deep longing, almost as if the wolf had been urging me to go wild, to join it.

For the briefest of moments, I could imagine what it must feel like to be a wild animal, a creature able to live in the wilderness with no need for tents and sleeping bags and backpacks and all that—to just be free and wild.

It made me want to cry. In fact, maybe I did cry a little, there in my tent, down deep inside my sleeping bag. I no longer wanted to go back to civilization, in spite of the weird happenings. I wanted to stay out on the trail forever. I wanted to be a wolf.

I finally drifted back to sleep, only to be awakened shortly afterwards by something pressing against my tent, large hands feeling around through the nylon sides. As the pressure came close to my head I quickly sat up, involuntarily shouting out. I then heard the sound of something very large running through the timber.

What the hey? I was totally puzzled, for I'd never heard of a bear doing anything like that, and it seemed to have had hands—and it had sounded bipedal as it ran. Was there some crazy hiker out here stealing stuff or worse yet, harming people?

I wasn't sure what to do. I really didn't want to break camp in the middle of the night, and there was no way I was going night hiking. But what if they came back? I knew it wasn't a bear, and even though I had bear spray, what if they had a gun?

I had no idea what time it was, but I knew there was no way I was going back to sleep. I would be a sitting duck. I wasn't sure what to do, but I felt an urgency that I needed to act quickly. It seemed my intuition was trying to wake me up and get me moving.

I always keep my pack in my tent alcove when sleeping, both to protect it from the elements and also to keep animals out of it. Since I carried only freeze-dried food most of the time, I wasn't too worried about it being near me and attracting bears.

So, I opened my tent door and dragged the pack inside, stuffed my sleeping bag into it, tied my sleeping pad on, then got myself dressed. Now my pack was ready, and I was all set to leave with everything but my tent.

I'd decided on the spur of the moment to hide. I would leave my tent there as a decoy, then go back into the trees and find a good spot to hunker down until morning. I could then go get my tent and make a beeline for Old Faithful.

If someone stole my tent, so be it, I was only one day from civilization and could either replace it or go home, the latter being my preference at that point. But there was no way I was going to stay inside it like the middle of an Oreo cookie, waiting for someone to come back and steal everything and who knows what.

I was quickly in the trees, keeping my headlamp off in case someone was watching. No point in tipping them off as to what I was doing.

It was hard going, as I kept tripping and running into branches, but I was finally far back to where I could no longer see the faint outline of my nylon tent in the starlight.

But I still didn't feel safe. I turned on my light for a brief second, just long enough to spot a big crooked tree that looked like it would hold my weight. I climbed up about 10 feet from the ground, hoisting my pack up behind me.

This would do. I felt much safer, for if someone did try to come up, I felt like I had a good defensible position. To my surprise, I could now see my tent's outline from my vantage point, though it was a ways off.

Now to try to stay as comfortable as possible and wait it out until morning. I leaned my back against the tree, flashing back on my military training, appreciative for the skills it had taught me. I knew that the secret to not being seen was to stay as still as possible.

Well, staying still is hard to do when every bone in your body is telling you to flee. And that's exactly what I wanted to do when I heard a sharp piercing whistle come from behind my tent, which was followed by another not too far to my right.

I've never known anybody who could whistle that loud, and you could tell it wasn't artificial, but was produced by something alive. And whatever it was, there were at least two of them.

I could now hear something walking heavily through the brush, not all that far from where I hid, and I held my breath, my heart in my throat. But it soon passed by, walking in the direction of the other whistle, towards my tent.

All was still for the longest time, then suddenly, from nowhere, I could hear someone talking really loud, agitated and angry, but I couldn't understand anything they were saying.

Another voice followed, and it, too, sounded angry. This was followed by what I can only describe as a maniacal screaming. I could now hear what sounded like stomping and ripping and the banging of tree limbs together, all accompanied by intermittent growling.

I could now see that the outline of my tent was gone. I had a sickening feeling that the ripping sound I'd heard was my tent being destroyed, and if you've ever tried to rip nylon, you know how hard that is.

I was right, whoever it was had come back looking for me, and upon discovering me gone, they were furious. I knew their next step was to start searching for me.

I wished that I'd gone further back into the trees, for I really wasn't all that far from where my tent had been, but it was too late. I knew that if I tried to flee, they would hear me, and I couldn't see well enough to go anywhere without my light, which would be a dead giveaway.

I tried to make myself smaller in the notch of the tree, but there was really nothing I could do but wait. I thought again of the two hikers I'd met on the trail and their reluctance to talk to me about what they'd seen. Maybe it was because they hadn't actually *seen* anything. I hadn't seen anything so far, and I didn't want to.

Now, I really can't explain what happened next, just like I can't explain any of the rest of this, but all of a sudden, it got deathly cold.

Remember, it was a nice August night, a typical night in Yellowstone where you're fine with just a light jacket. But now it was cold, and I mean so cold I started shivering. It was the kind of unnatural cold you feel when you put your hand near a block of dry ice.

I was starting to have trouble breathing, and now I could smell rotten eggs, and I immediately felt nauseous. I could hear coughing and gagging over by where my tent had been, then everything went quiet.

As my throat started to constrict, I recalled something I'd read once about some employees in Yellowstone digging a deep pit for some reason or other, way back in the 1930s.

One of the guys fell ill while in the pit, and the other tried to pull him out, but fell into the pit himself. Both were rescued, but neither was ever the same afterwards. What had happened to them? I tried to remember, but my thinking was getting fuzzier and fuzzier.

Suddenly, it came to me. Hydrogen sulfide gas! The Yellowstone geysers often emit H2S, or hydrogen sulfide, which is deadly when it becomes concentrated in low areas.

It smells like rotten eggs, though the longer you're around it, the less you can smell it, as it deadens your sense of smell. Exposure can make you stop breathing and die.

I couldn't hear any sounds coming from over by my tent, and I suspected the H2S was stronger over there. Maybe they'd collapsed! In any case, I had to get out of there immediately, as I knew I risked dying.

I could already feel the effects of the gas, for when I tried to slip from the tree I was sluggish and uncoordinated, almost falling. I quickly turned on my headlamp and found the trail, then headed back towards the park boundary, returning the way I'd come.

The trail followed the lake for awhile, then immediately entered the deadfall area, where I had no trouble following it with my bright light. I went as fast as I reasonably could without risking breaking something, glad I'd taken the time to filter some water the previous evening. It would be a long hike back, assuming I made it.

The further I got from the lake, the better I started to feel—both physically and mentally. It didn't seem like I was being followed, and I knew it had to soon be dawn. I grabbed some nuts from my pack and ate as I walked along, slowly regaining my strength, though my throat still hurt.

I could see the first hints of light as I stopped for a drink and a quick break. I was beginning to be able to see the trail without my light.

As I sat on a log, I tried to understand what had happened. I didn't think H2S gas would be cold like that, so was the cold from something else? And had the creatures back there succumbed to it? Would I have died from the gas if I hadn't left my tent? Was I now being careless by stopping and thinking they weren't following me? What exactly were they, anyway?

I was beginning to wonder if I hadn't dreamed it all when I heard a distant wavering call, long and mournful, which was then joined by a second voice. I at first thought it was wolves, but it continued on and on, so long that I knew it couldn't be any kind of small animal.

It was far behind me, maybe even still back at Summit Lake, but I knew the things were still alive and I needed to get going as fast as I could. Did they know which direction I'd gone? Or was it possibly others who'd discovered the bodies of the first ones?

It was then that I almost jumped out of my skin as another thru-hiker came upon me. He'd gotten an early start on the trail and looked happy and carefree, probably because he knew he would soon be at Old Faithful and could get a hot meal and shower.

I didn't know what to say. I wanted to warn him off, but I knew he would think I was crazy.

Finally, I said, "You might want to hike out this way with me." I was eager to get going.

"Why?" he asked, perplexed.

"There's weirdness back there," I answered. "Look, just come on out with me. There's something back in there that you really don't want to meet."

"A bear?" he asked, concerned.

"No, not a bear. Look, I gotta get going. Just turn around and hike out."

He shook his head and said, "Hey, we each gotta hike our own hike. Good luck and see you down the trail."

To this day, I have no idea if he made it on through or not, nor do I know if anyone ever found what I assume were the remains of my tent. I do know that there are people who have gone missing in the park and its environs, and I know there are things I can't explain.

I finally made it to a place where I could get on the highway and hitch a ride, and I ended up in Bozeman, Montana, thanks to you giving me a ride, Rusty. And as you know, I got a bus ticket home, where I spent the next few months happily doing handyman work through the winter.

When spring rolled around, I once again began to feel that wanderlust that had led me to become a thru-hiker, but instead of getting back on the trail, I bought a pickup with a camper and went down in the Black Hills, close to home.

I'll admit to a few nights where, even in my camper, I was scared to death, just thinking about my time on the CDT in Yellowstone, but all in all, I enjoyed the camping. And that's when I got the invite to come hang out with you guys, which I really appreciate.

They say to hike you own hike, and my hike is now mostly to the river to fish, and that's what makes me happy. And I now like to have others around, loner that I once was.

So, my philosophy now is still to hike your own hike, but just be sure it's a hike you can finish.

8

THE TRANQUIL BIGFOOT

The following story first appeared in my book, Mysterious Bigfoot Campfire Stories. I'm including it here since it's near Yellowstone.

I met the fellow who told the following story out near Gardiner, Montana. He was driving a government truck and saw me fishing the Yellowstone River and stopped to talk. I'll never forget the story he told, even though it took quite a bit of conversation before he felt comfortable enough with me to tell it.

It's a good one, and I must say he's not the first person I've met who believes Bigfoot wanders Yellowstone National Park, even though this incident took place not far out of the park boundary.

So be careful when you come up to one of those remote hot springs— you might just surprise one of the big guys having a good soak—Rusty

I'm a wildlife biologist. When people find this out, they always think I lead a life of outdoor adventure, which is actually rarely the case. I probably spend more time indoors in an office writing up reports and doing surveys than I do outdoors, especially in the winter.

But there was one time that I bet few can match for excitement, or maybe I should call it adventure—or maybe there are better words for that day, such as disbelief, wonder, and terror.

And believe me, none of my scientific colleagues know this story —well, with one exception—a fellow employee who is sworn to secrecy. I know she'll keep her pledge since she saw the same thing once.

It was early winter, and I was out in the forest trying to do a wolf count. This happened in the Yellowstone Park area, not far from the Lamar Valley, where packs of wolves tend to hang out. I worked for a state agency, not the park, but I can't say any more about that—it would be too easy to figure out who I am, as I still work there.

I carried a dart gun with tranquilizer darts because there was a lone wolf, a female, that I wanted to radio collar. Normally one would never do this kind of work alone, but there just wasn't anyone else available to go out with me. I really wanted to be able to collar this particular wolf if I happened to come across her, which was unlikely. But I wanted to be ready, just in case.

Winter is a good time to observe wildlife in the Yellowstone area as the grizzly bears are hibernating and not a problem. Otherwise, one has to be really cautious. But in winter, about all you have to worry about are the bison, and they aren't much of a worry, really, as they stick together and you can easily avoid the herds.

So, I was creeping along in the cover of the trees on the edge of a valley, stopping all the time to use my binoculars and scout around. A few times I saw movement down by the river, but it always turned out to be coyotes.

I came across a beautiful herd of bison in the distance, but nothing really unusual. It was a cold crisp day with sunny blue skies, perfect weather for what I was doing, and I was really enjoying myself. I really liked my job when I wasn't stuck indoors.

I slowly snowshoed along the small valley I was in, staying at the edge of the trees, stopping a lot to scope things out, looking for wolves. The snow was only a foot or so deep, so the going was easy. I felt like a mountain man, as I had the whole place to myself—well, me and the animals.

I carried a daypack with my lunch and a thermos of hot tea with lots of sugar for energy, and I finally decided it was time to sit down on a rock and enjoy a bite to eat. I was on a rise, and a breeze had picked up and was cooling things down, but it was still pretty nice if you sat in the direct sun. But even though it was only about one p.m., I knew I only had another couple of hours before I needed to head back, as the sun set by five and I was a good hour or so in.

I finished my sandwich and was sipping some hot tea from my thermos when I noticed what looked like a pair of wolves across the valley. I was excited, and quickly got out my binoculars.

Sure enough, it was a wolf pair, and I forgot all about my tea, watching them with a thrill. I had helped collar some of the wolves in the area and had subsequently developed a great interest in their well-being, but I didn't recognize this pair.

They were nonchalantly walking along the edge of the forest, heading for the river, probably on their way for a drink. Sure enough, they were soon at the water, drinking. As I watched, I suddenly heard a strange noise coming from the forest downhill from me, on my side of the river. It sounded like something big moaning in pain.

The wolves stopped in their tracks and looked up at where the noise was coming from, paused for a brief moment, then skedaddled back into the forest they'd come from, not wasting any time, loping along and kind of looking over their shoulders. They soon disappeared into the thick timber.

Well, this gave me pause, because there's not much that a wolf is afraid of. In fact, I'm not sure there's anything, except humans, and they didn't seem to be aware of me. Whatever had made that sound had scared them.

I sat there, wondering what was going on, when I heard it again. It was definitely an animal in distress, and it sounded like something big. I wondered what was going on, my instincts telling me it was time to go home.

I usually listen carefully to my instincts, especially after spending so much time in a wilderness that has plenty of apex predators, but for some reason my curiosity overran my fears. After all, I was a wildlife biologist, and I was wondering what kind of animal would make a sound like that. I knew all the bears were in hibernation. Was there a wounded bison over there? That's about all I could figure could make such a deep moaning sound. I had never heard anything like it.

I've seen wounded animals before, and I knew better than to get near them, but I guess my tranquilizer gun gave me a sort of false bravado. If there were a wounded animal nearby, my training said not to mess with it, to just let nature take its course, but my scientific curiosity got the better of me. I also carried a rifle—a 30.06—so if worse came to worse, I could shoot it and put it out of its misery. I hated to see anything suffer.

I decided that I would carefully skirt over there and see what it was, be extra cautious, then head back to my truck. It couldn't be all that far over to where the sound had come from, and it was on my side of the river. I put my pack back on and felt like I was prepared for whatever it was.

Well, I wasn't prepared at all, I found out.

As I quietly skirted the trees, the moaning sounded out again, and it was truly heart rending. It almost sounded human, and I stopped. What if it was a human? That would explain why the wolves had fled —in fact, that's about the only explanation I could come up with.

But a human could never make a sound that loud. It was a deep and distinct sound, something more like a bison or large animal would make, and it almost shook the ground I was standing on. I was puzzled, but again continued, walking very quietly and watching where I put my feet so as to not step on branches and alert it.

The creature moaned again and again, each time giving me pause and making me want to flee, but also showing me where it was, like a directional beacon. Because I was going so slow, it took me quite a while to get to it, but when I did, I felt like someone must feel who discovers a new species.

I had crept in behind some big rocks, and when I got the courage to peek around them, I was shocked beyond words.

There, lying on the ground on its side as if it were too weak to fight anymore, was a man-like being about the size of a human teenager, but covered from head to toe in slick reddish-brown hair. Its back was to me, but I could see it had something wrong with it. It was partially hidden behind some shrubs so that I couldn't quite make out what was going on.

Now the creature raised itself on its elbows and moaned again, the immensity of the sound taking my breath away. Whatever it was, it had one good pair of lungs. The sound was way louder than one would expect from something that size.

It now tried to scoot itself along on its hips, then stopped, obviously in pain and somehow weighed down. Did it have a broken leg or something? If so, I would be obligated to shoot it. But how could I shoot something that seemed so human?

I was pondering what to do more than trying to figure out what it was, which I did later—in fact, I became obsessed with trying to classify it. I tried to get a better vantage point, but I just couldn't see what was the matter.

I stood there, hidden, for some time, not sure what to do. I was thinking it was a monkey or gorilla of some kind, but I had no idea why it would be in the wilds near Yellowstone. Maybe it had escaped some private zoo. You know how your mind tries to make sense of something it can't figure out, something so foreign that it makes no sense to you, so you just keep mulling it over and over.

I knew I had to do something and couldn't just stand there any longer, so I inched my way around to where I could see better. I was still behind it, but I could now see that its foot was caught in some kind of trap. It looked to be an old bear trap of some kind and looked all rusted out.

The creature would try to pull off the trap with its big hands, then moan from the pain, unsuccessful. I had no idea how long it had been there, but there was blood on its foot and all around on the snow, so I knew it had been trapped for some time, bleeding. I felt sick thinking of the pain it must be in, as the huge jaws of the trap looked pretty well entrenched in the flesh of its foot.

I knew there was no way I could help it without getting up close to it to spring the trap. I'd come across animals in traps before, but never in the park, as it was totally illegal to trap there. I'd always had someone with me to help, and we would generally either tranquilize and release it or shoot the animal if there was nothing we could do.

I got out my tranquilizer gun. I would just have to tranquilize it and release it and let it go on its way to recovery or death, but that was all I could do.

I put my gun to my shoulder and shot a dart into its back between the shoulder blades where it couldn't reach it. The animal jumped, startled. I knew the darts had to sting a bit, but not too bad. It turned towards me, but couldn't move enough to look my way.

After a while, I knew I needed a second dart, so I reloaded and shot it again, then waited some more, trying to quit shaking. Now the animal was nodding its head down onto its chest, and I knew it was time to move in. I had no idea how long the effect would last on something this big, as the largest animal I'd ever tranquilized was a wolf.

I very cautiously moved closer, picking up a long stick, then poking it a bit to see if it would react. It didn't, so I quickly went to the trap and was able to spring it, though it was difficult. The trap was old and rusted, and I guess it had been set many years ago. The poor creature had unwarily stepped into it.

I pulled the big teeth of the trap away from the creature's flesh, which wasn't easy, as it had dug deep. I didn't want to contribute to the damage, but I had to get it off.

The foot was a mess, and I felt really bad for the animal. I had no idea if it could survive this, and even if it did, if it would be able to walk again and forage or hunt for food and water. I was again tempted to just shoot it and put it out of its misery, but it just seemed wrong. Keep in mind that I hadn't seen its face at this point, as I was too busy springing the trap.

I got up and went back to where I'd left my pack by the rocks, getting out my first-aid kit. It had only a few essentials in it, but one of those was a small bottle of iodine. All government field employees in my region had to take first-aid courses, so I had an idea of what to do.

I tried to clean out the wound a bit and then poured the whole bottle onto it, hoping it would help keep it from getting infected. I wondered if I should wrap it, but I decided the creature would just take it all off.

Now I had to get out of there, as there was no more I could do, and who knew how long I had before the animal woke up. As I stood to go, I saw it move a bit. Its head had been resting on its left cheek, turned away from me, but now I saw it had turned its head back and its eyes were open, watching me.

I could now see its face, and I was stunned. It looked exactly like a human, but with a larger brow and a flat nose, and of course, it was much bigger. Its eyes were glazed with the sedative, but I knew it was awake enough to know what was going on. It watched me intently, and I immediately stepped back, then turned and ran like hell in sheer shock and fear as I realized what I was seeing.

I had never seen anything like it, and I hoped I never would again. All I know is I picked up my gear and ran as fast as my legs would carry me on snowshoes until I had to slow down because my lungs were burning in pain. I was too scared to even look back, but I could imagine it at my heels, which in retrospect was unlikely, given its condition.

It was almost dark when I got back to my truck, threw my pack onto the front seat, and jumped in, looking over my shoulder the whole time. I drove as fast as prudent back down the long and rough slick road.

I took the next week off, saying I was ill. I couldn't sleep at night, and I kept thinking something was trying to break into my house. I would dream strange shadowy dreams of manlike beasts trying to get me, large dark monsters limping through my back pasture and coming to the house and trying to break in.

Finally, after a week, my mind started calming down a bit, even though I was still in somewhat of a state of shock. I returned to work, but I told my boss I couldn't do any more wolf counts for a while as I was still too sick.

I ended up taking several months of leave without pay and spending time with my cousin at his place in Bozeman, Montana, recovering my balance. I had no idea such a creature existed, and I was too embarrassed to even talk about it to anyone, as I didn't want people to think I was going insane.

Finally, I returned to work, and months later, I was taking a coffee break with a fellow employee who had been out in the field the previous week doing the wolf work I had been assigned but couldn't do.

She informed me she was going to ask for a transfer because she wanted to go to some place warmer. This really shocked me, as I had thought working with wolves was one of her life dreams. I suspected something had happened.

I flat out asked if she'd seen something unusual. She looked at me kind of funny, but refused to talk about it. I decided to tell her about my experience, and she listened intently.

Finally, she started sobbing and shaking. I tried to reassure her, and it was then that she told me what she'd seen, not more than a month after I'd seen it.

Not far from where I'd taken off the trap, over on the other side of the valley, she'd been sitting in the trees watching for wolves and had instead seen a dark creature walk on two legs down to the river where it bent down and drank. It then stood, looked directly her way, and started towards her.

She had panicked and was ready to run when it turned and walked the other way. She quickly retreated, running to her truck, just as I had done, scared to death.

We talked about it for a while, both agreeing it had to be a Bigfoot. And sure enough, it had a limp, but seemed otherwise fine.

I have no idea if it realized I'd saved its life and was thereby disposed favorably towards humans, or if it also realized that a human had made the trap that almost cost it its life. I'll never know, but my co-worker decided to stay, though neither of us will work in that area without someone else with us.

We later found out that one of Yellowstone's most prominent backcountry rangers had seen these beasts numerous times in the park and firmly believed in them, going on the record after he'd quit his job.

So I guess we're not nuts after all.

9

THE YELLOWSTONE WHISPERS

The following story first appeared in my book, Bigfoot: The Dark Side. I'm including it here since it happened in Yellowstone.

Winston was part of a group I met while teaching an introductory class in fly-fishing near my home base of Steamboat Springs, Colorado. He was a quiet guy at first, but turned out to be quite a storyteller over the campfire after one of my famous dutch-oven dinners.

Everyone in the group really took to him, and we all listened in rapt silence as he told the following story over the hot coals of the dying fire. Even though we weren't far out in the wilds and fairly close to town, I swear we were half-afraid to leave the firelight when he was done. —Rusty

Well, Rusty, I'm a bit older now, but I was in my 50s when this happened. I'm kind of ashamed to say it took me over half a century to open my eyes to the world around me, but as they say, better late than never.

The incident I'm about to relate was indeed an eye-opener for me, and I probably learned more about life from it than I did in all my preceding years.

I know you've been to Yellowstone, but a lot of people haven't, and even among those who have, a lot of them don't realize just how huge the place really is.

It's an incredible landscape, very little of which is ever actually visited by people, even by those who get out and hike the back-country trails. There's just so much timber, and a lot of it is so thick you can barely bushwhack your way through it. There's no hunting, and because it's grizzly bear habitat, a lot of people won't hike the interior, and so, it's the perfect habitat for...well, I'll get to that soon.

But my age, that's part of the story. When you get to be middle-aged and you work for a corporation, they often don't see you as an asset, but instead, tend to look at you as someone who is nearing retirement. If they can get rid of you before you retire and qualify for your full pension, they can save a bundle of money.

But they have to do it in a manner that won't come back and bite them on the rear end. They have to make it look like they're down-sizing the company or something like that—they can't be discrimina-tory because of your age—at least in theory, anyway.

To make things worse, I worked in IT as a manager. Computer technology is probably one of the worst jobs you can have these days. It used to be a very secure position, but now you have to stay on top of a lot of new stuff, and it's really easy to lose your job to some guy in India. Managers are easy to replace, usually by someone who will work cheaper.

I knew all this, and I knew the writing was on the wall, but I only had two years left until I could retire, and I really hoped I could make it. But the day my manager called me into her office, I had a sinking feeling it was all over, and I was right.

I did manage to negotiate a payout, which wasn't a whole lot. It was about one-half of my annual salary, but it did give me a bit of a buffer until I could figure out what to do next. I would also get a pension, but it wouldn't be much.

What to do? I had no idea, but I knew I needed a change in my life. I was sick of working in a cubicle, and my health had taken a turn for the worse because of my lack of exercise and poor eating habits. I was divorced, no kids, so at least I had no responsibilities except for myself, which was good.

I'll never forget the day I got laid off. I went back to my small apartment and sat there, looking around at the stuff I'd managed to accumulate, kind of in shock.

Twenty-four hours later, that apartment was almost empty. I'd called Habitat for Humanity, who came and took away almost everything to their store. Since that's where I'd gotten most of it anyway, I felt that was appropriate.

I took most of my clothes to the thrift store, as well as my dishes and kitchen stuff. I then went down to the local outdoors store where I told them I was going backpacking in Yellowstone, and I'd soon dropped a nice chunk of change on equipment, which included two canisters of bear spray.

This story is going to be long anyway, so I'll cut to the chase. Forty-eight hours after closing down my apartment, I was in Yellowstone. I don't even remember the drive, except for the emotions I went through, which included shock, bitterness, anger, and excitement.

Why Yellowstone? I'm not really sure. Maybe I'd read it was a good place to get out into the wilderness. I'd never been there, and I had no idea where to go or what to do once I was there.

I couldn't have cared less about seeing the geysers and tourist sites, I was there to run away and hide in the deepest wilderness I could find. I wanted time and space to process everything and decide what to do next. In retrospect, I really had no idea what I was doing. I was being compulsive, I guess, mostly from fear.

But there I was, in Yellowstone National Park. I went into the Visitor Center and got some maps and information and found out that I needed a backcountry permit. This included watching a mandatory video about bear safety. I'd chosen an area of the park where few people go, so it was easy to get a permit.

I didn't know diddly squat about anything, I just knew I needed to get away, even though the ranger I talked to was concerned that I was going out alone, saying that bears are more bold around solo hikers. He said that as a solo backpacker, I really should stay where there were more people, especially since I was new to it all. But I was dead set on being out where there were few people, and I was soon on my way to the trailhead.

Once there, I loaded all my gear into the backpack. The guy at the outdoor store had been really helpful, and I felt like I was pretty much prepared for anything. I had enough freeze-dried food for two weeks, a water filter, rain gear, new boots, and a hammock, which the guy at the store said would be much easier to carry than a tent. I also had a small tarp that I could use if it rained.

All this, along with some cooking gear and a few other things, pretty much made for a full pack—oh, and I even had the required bear-proof storage canister.

Once at the trailhead, I was the only car in the parking lot, which surprised me somewhat, but that's why I was there, because I wanted to get away from people. I will admit that the complete lack of anyone else around made me a bit nervous, as I'd expected to see at least another car or two.

Let me say that I am purposely being vague, as I don't really want to disclose the area where all this happened. I definitely don't want to encourage people to go there, and after reading this account, I know there are people who would try to find where this happened. I don't want to be a part of anyone getting injured, or maybe worse.

I've followed the Yellowstone news since this trip, and I've seen some really odd and mysterious reports, but they are few and far between. I truly think the rangers are trying to keep a lid on all this, and I also think they're probably right to do so. From the talk I had with the ranger at the end of my adventure (or maybe I should call it my misadventure), I can't help but think they know exactly what's going on, even though they probably don't understand it—but I don't think anyone does.

Anyway, I hoisted my pack onto my back and headed up the trail. This was not only my first time backpacking, but it was one of the few times I'd ever gone hiking. Living in the city makes it hard to get very far away, especially when you work all the time, like I had.

I immediately began worrying. What if I ran into a bear? What if I got lost? What if I was so out of shape that I twisted my ankle or worse? At my age, and in as poor condition as I was, even a heart attack could be a possibility. Ironically, I wasn't even aware that the thing that proved to be my greatest danger even existed.

But the further I got up the trail, the more my worries faded away. I was too busy huffing and puffing to worry about anything, as well as trying to adjust my pack so it would stop hurting my shoulders. I moved slow and was soon lost in the beauty around me, the silence broken only by the sound of my own breathing and the call of a pair of ravens.

Ravens. I knew nothing about the species, but I found them intriguing. They followed me, landing in the trees nearby and making all kinds of noise. I found them to be good company, and they made me forget my fears.

Little did I know that ravens aid and abet predators by advertising where prey is, hoping to make good on a free meal after the bear or mountain lion has made the kill and had their fill. If I'd known that, I would've chased them off, thrown rocks at them, whatever it took.

Instead, in my innocence and ignorance, I laughed and felt like I was special for them to pay me so much attention. I later realized how ignorant of the wilds I was, an ignorance that could have easily cost me my life—well, an ignorance that actually almost *did* cost me my life.

The trail didn't climb much, but instead wound through a long beautiful meadow. It was perfect for acclimating myself to the pack and setting a pace. I soon quit huffing and puffing and began to get my stride.

I was in a new world, the most beautiful and primal place I'd ever been. I immediately understood why people became so passionate about nature. I felt sad that I'd spent most of my life in the city. I was in my 50s and only now had discovered how great it felt to get away from it all.

Oh well, I thought, maybe it was for the best. If I'd known about this earlier, I probably would've quit my job and become a guide or something, then so much for having a good retirement.

The irony of it all hit me. I'd pretty much wasted my life, given it to a corporation, and now the only retirement I would have other than my small pension would be social security, and I wouldn't qualify for that for a number of years. I would've been better off in the long run going hiking every day—at least I would be in good shape, which I wasn't now. The thought was discouraging, and I stopped to take a break and sit on a large rock.

I took out a package of M&Ms and ate them as the ravens came near, curious. I almost threw them a few, but I knew it was illegal to feed wildlife in the park, plus I wasn't sure if ravens could eat chocolate—maybe it was poisonous to them, like it was to dogs.

I suddenly wished I had a dog, knowing I'd feel safer, though I knew I wouldn't be able to bring it hiking in the park. Maybe I would get a dog when I got home. It then struck me that I had no home, no place to go.

I sighed. I guessed I would just make Yellowstone my home, at least for the next two weeks. I would deal with the future when I had to. Maybe I'd make the Tetons my next home after this. Then I could call Glacier National Park home for a few weeks.

It gradually dawned on me that I really didn't need a home—I could live out of my car and backpack. I could go south in the winter and north in the summer. It would be a cheap way to live, and I could probably survive on my savings for a couple of years, if not longer, as all I would need was food and gas. Imagine the kind of shape I'd be in!

Maybe I should go to all the parks. That was it! I would spend the next few years trying to visit every national park in the U.S.

I felt energized, maybe from the sugar, but also from the thought of being free. I was soon back on the trail, a spring in my step, my whole outlook changed.

But it didn't take long for the excitement to wane, as I could feel the distance from my car and from civilization with every step, and the worrying soon returned. Keep in mind that I was as unfamiliar with the wilds as a city boy could be, and such unfamiliarity bred hesitation and fear.

I think some fear is probably healthy, as we need to be aware of our surroundings, yet I also recognized that my particular fears were probably misguided, as there was nothing out here that would harm me—other than a grizzly bear or two, maybe.

But suddenly my fears were becoming reality, as I could hear the crunch-crunch sound of something coming down the trail, something really big!

I was terrified and did the opposite of what the Visitor Center movie said to do—instead of making myself known so as to not surprise a bear, I stepped off the trail and hid behind some thick bushes. I knew bears have an incredible sense of smell, but somehow I thought it wouldn't know I was there and would keep on going.

I stood for a moment, scared to death, as sure enough, something really big and dark came down the trail. It paused, then stepped into sight, and I knew it could smell me, for it stopped right next to where I was hidden, swinging its head back and forth and snorting.

A buffalo, or, more accurately, a bison! The thing was huge, and I realized it was probably every bit as dangerous as a bear, maybe even more so. And to make things worse, there were several more behind it!

I tried to reach for my bear spray, but couldn't get to the side pocket in my pack. I realized that this was a real rookie mistake that might cost me my life. All I could do was stand quietly and wait.

After a moment, the bison continued on down the trail, the others following, paying me no mind. I then realized that if it had been a bear, I probably wouldn't have even heard it coming, for bears walk much more quietly.

The bison were soon gone, and I started breathing again, slipped off my pack, put both cans of bear spray in more accessible pockets, then headed back up the trail, feeling shaky.

My first wildlife encounter in Yellowstone had gone pretty well, all things considered. I knew that this would be part of the store of experience that I would gradually build up until I felt more comfortable in the backcountry, and hopefully none of that experience would kill me. I knew that two weeks of this would make me a much more adept and confident backpacker, though I still would be a rookie. Nothing like doing one's first backpack trip in one of the wildest places in America.

I stopped again, resting on a log, wondering how far I'd hiked. I pulled out the map and realized I'd gone maybe a mile at the most. I could already feel my shoulders seizing up from the heavy pack, and my knees were starting to hurt.

At that rate, I'd be lucky to even get a few miles before I'd have to make my first camp. I felt discouraged, but soon realized it just didn't matter. I was free to go when and where I wanted, and if I hiked 100 feet a day, that was fine. I was here to enjoy the wilds and regroup, not set any hiking records. I would start a new life and get in shape along the way.

On the other hand, it was somewhat comforting to know my car wasn't all that far away, so I wasn't really that disappointed to not have gone far.

I was totally alone in the wilds, and I have to admit I was still on edge and fearful. I even toyed with the idea of going back and finding a spot in one of the park's campgrounds, surrounded by people.

But to my credit, I kept going—maybe I wasn't as big of a coward as I'd feared. The ravens had left, and the forest was now very quiet. It began to take on an almost ominous feeling, like before a big storm hits, though the weather forecast had called for good weather.

I instinctively looked to the sky, half expecting to see huge thunderheads forming, but it was a marvelous blue, a color like I'd never seen in the city. In spite of the quiet and tenseness, I felt elated to be there.

I managed to hike another mile or so, then decided it would be prudent to stop for the day and make camp. It was only mid-afternoon, but I was tired, and I knew it would take me awhile to get camp set up, as it was my first time. No reason to push it.

I hadn't seen hide nor hair of another human, which was fine by me. The trail skirted a small meadow, which looked to be perfect for my first camp. There were a few trees that would make a good place to hang my hammock, providing I could remember how to do it.

It felt good to take off the heavy pack, and I soon had the hammock hung and was resting in it. It was beyond comfortable, and before I knew it, I was waking to a fiery sunset through the trees. I had no idea what time it was, but I knew I'd slept for several hours.

I hurried and set up my little stove and soon had dinner going, a freeze-dried stew with apple crumb for dessert. I was famished and now understood why people said food tasted so much better in the outdoors. I was also very thirsty and drank one of the four water bottles I carried. I wasn't worried about refilling it, as the ranger had said water was plentiful in this area. I would have to filter whatever I found, but it was no big deal.

Now with a restful nap and dinner behind me, I felt much better, and I was soon leaning back in the hammock watching the stars come out.

I'll never forget that first night out—it was so incredibly beautiful and peaceful. Later, after what I went through, I would often remember how that first night out was so different from what was to come.

But then, ignorance is bliss, as they say.

The Greater Yellowstone Ecosystem is one of the wildest and least-touched places in the U.S. In my ignorance, I had no idea that unknown creatures could exist there, unnoticed and undetected. I think that next time I'll go to someplace less remote to find myself— but I'm getting ahead of the story.

Even though I'd slept for several hours, I was still exhausted, but I wanted to stay awake to enjoy the starry sky. I knew it would be a sight like I'd never seen before and would include my first time seeing the Milky Way. But I was soon fast asleep, dead to the world around me, which may not have been so wise given where I was.

We humans can't see very well in the dark, so it's important that we're protected as best can be at night, especially when sleeping in a hammock, which is actually quite exposed—at the very least, one should have a headlamp and bear spray handy. I had neither, leaving both in my pack.

But I guess my senses were still on partial alert, as something did wake me, though I had no idea what—I just knew I was suddenly wide awake from a deep sleep.

I lay very still, listening, but all was quiet. I finally decided I'd awakened because I'd forgotten to put my food in the bear canister. I fumbled around and found my headlamp, put my food away, and tidied camp a bit, then climbed back into my hammock, tucking my headlamp and bear spray into the hammock's side pocket. The slight swaying soon made me nod off again, but it was short-lived, as I again awoke.

I'd heard something, but what? It had to be a strange noise to wake me, but then, everything out here was a strange noise to my city ears. Once again, I lay still, listening, but now getting more and more fearful. What if it was a bear? I slowly pulled out the bear spray and held it ready.

Now I could hear what sounded like children laughing, though far in the distance. I wasn't that far from the trailhead, and perhaps a young family had hiked in behind me and camped nearby.

And even though it seemed odd that young children would be up in the middle of the night, it gave me a sense of comfort, knowing there were others nearby. Soon, the laughter faded into the distance, turning into a whispering sound as if the wind was moving through the forest. I soon fell back asleep.

I woke at dawn, the bear spray resting on my chest, tiny birds flitting around and chirping in the trees above. It took awhile to wake up, and I first thought I was back in my apartment and couldn't make sense of anything, especially the birds, but I eventually realized where I was.

I was soon up, making coffee and a freeze-dried packet of scrambled eggs. I was again famished, and I followed the eggs down with two granola bars and some raisins, then made yet another package of eggs.

Man, at this rate, I would run out of food in a week. I would just have to be sure I didn't get too far out so I could return in short order if I needed to, though at the speed I was going, that wouldn't be much of a concern.

I lazed around in my hammock, sore but happy. I was in the most beautiful of places, and the worries of the previous day were forgotten, though I still wondered why children would be playing during the night.

It was mid-morning before I had my pack ready and again hit the trail. Today I would keep an eye out for water, as I'd already used half of what I was carrying. I would also keep an eye out for the family I'd heard during the night, as it would be nice to see others out here. Maybe I could even hike with them a ways.

I found I was almost too sore to continue, but as the day wore on, I kind of walked it out and felt better, though I did stop a lot to rest. Once again, my appetite got the better of me, and I stopped mid-day to make a packet of freeze-dried spaghetti. So much for losing all my flab, though I knew I was burning a lot of calories.

I never did see the family I'd heard during the night, and as I got deeper and deeper into the wilds, I vacillated between pure elation and sheer panic. Fortunately, the elation usually won out, and the feelings of panic gradually subsided.

I felt like I was getting used to this new life, this new wilderness environment, the one we humans had originally called home long before we habituated ourselves to city life like a bunch of scurrying ants.

Before long, just like the ranger had predicted, I came upon a small stream. I stopped and filtered water, which took much longer than I had anticipated. I then continued on up the trail until I could see what looked like steam rising through the trees. I knew I had to be nearing some of Yellowstone's thermal activity.

Although Yellowstone is famous for its large geysers, such as Old Faithful, a lot of the park is dotted with hot pools and small geysers. These are a delight to the numerous bison and other wildlife during the winter, as the heat helps mitigate the extremely cold temperatures in the park. In the summer, the hot pools are a delight to people like myself, who enjoy bathing their tired aching bodies in the water, as long as it's not too hot.

I veered off-trail and headed towards the steam, excited. I was so sore that the thought of dangling my feet in warm water sounded heavenly.

Sure enough, I was soon at several hot pools with a small stream running through them. I hoped the stream would mellow out the boiling thermal waters enough to bathe in.

I quickly had my boots off and was soaking my feet in the warm water. It was indeed heavenly. Even though I hadn't come more than a few miles, I knew this would be my next camp.

I was soon stripped-down and immersed up to my neck in the warm waters, feeling like I'd found paradise, my sore muscles relaxing.

So far, I was thoroughly enchanted with Yellowstone. My city woes were far behind, and I would've been hard pressed to tell you even what city I'd lived in, though it hadn't been that long ago.

I spent the entire rest of the day there, finally forcing myself to get out of the water before I wrinkled up, it felt so good. I found a couple of trees that were perfect for my hammock, then got out my cooking gear. Still hungry, I made myself another dinner, following that with a hot cup of tea and an apple.

It was now evening, and I noticed movement in the trees beyond the small meadow with the hot pools. There was something dark back in there, and I reached for my bear spray. Before long, the dark figures had moved out from the forest to where I could see them.

Once again, it was bison, a small group of six, and I knew they wanted to come to the water. They seemed wary because I was there, for they stood looking in my direction. I decided to walk back into the woods a ways, giving them space enough to come and drink.

Still carrying the bear spray, I slipped back into the trees, pushing my way through thick undergrowth until I came upon an animal trail that wound through the forest.

Near the trail was a small clearing in the undergrowth, and I soon realized that it was probably a place where bears bedded down during the day. I was instantly on alert, and even more so when I saw several large bear tracks on the trail ahead of me. They were the first I'd ever seen, and I marveled at how large they were, though I couldn't help but shiver.

I decided I should go back to camp, as the last thing I wanted was an encounter with a grizzly. But as I turned around, I saw something quickly slip off the trail into the trees. It had been no more than 30 feet behind me! I felt a surge of adrenaline.

Whatever it was, it was large and dark, so I figured it was a black bear. It certainly was quiet, I noted as I pushed my way back through the undergrowth in panic, making lots of noise. The Visitor Center movie had talked about how fast bears can run, but it hadn't said anything about a bear following someone, especially so quietly.

I stopped at the edge of the forest to check on the bison, which were now drinking from the stream, but they suddenly turned and stampeded.

Had I frightened them? It didn't seem likely, as I hadn't yet stepped from the trees where they could see me. Bison have a reputation for being fearless, and I'd read about a woman who'd been stomped to death by one in Teddy Roosevelt National Park. Yellowstone tourists also frequently had encounters with them, occasionally fatal. I was actually surprised that my presence earlier had made them fearful enough to not come to the stream.

I then realized that the bear that I'd seen on the trail had probably frightened the herd. Would a bear cause them to stampede like that? Something didn't feel quite right. Were bison really that afraid of bears? Were there hunters around? No, it wasn't the right time of year, and besides, there's no hunting in national parks.

I thought it would probably be prudent to move camp, especially seeing how close I was to a bear trail, but I was just so exhausted that doing so didn't seem possible. Soaking in the hot water had turned me into a limp noodle, and I'd already been tired when I'd arrived.

The thought was too much, so I tidied up camp, then crawled into my sleeping bag in my hammock to watch the sunset, too tired to worry about much.

The sunset was fiery beyond anything I'd ever seen, yet I was too fatigued to even get my camera out for a photo.

I drifted off, tired to the bone, but again awoke in the middle of the night to children's laughter. As before, it seemed distant, so I listened for awhile, then went back to sleep, thinking the family was again nearby. It made sense that they would be progressing up the trail at about my speed if they had young children with them. Why they were so noisy at night was beyond me, but I was soon back asleep.

I suddenly woke in a panic. I felt as if I were in the middle of a circle of strange creatures all whispering at once, whispering loud like the wind. My hammock began swaying, and the rational part of my mind said it had to be the wind, though I somehow knew it was the strange creatures.

And as I lay there, my hammock swaying more and more, I remembered reading long ago about the Yellowstone Whispers. Try as I might, I couldn't remember much besides that people would hear a strange whispering sound in Yellowstone, even though it would be a calm day or night.

But now something was trying to strangle me! I could feel huge hands around my neck holding me down, trying to cut off my air. And now the whispering grew even louder. I began struggling, and the hands let go.

Now my hammock stopped swaying, the whispering stopped, and I began to realize it was a dream, even though it felt real. I lifted myself up and looked around. There was nothing there.

I could see it was morning, and I was surrounded by a thick fog, my down sleeping bag soaked to the gills. Wet and chilly, I swung from my hammock and quickly pulled the tarp from my pack, trying to make a shelter, but soon gave up. It was too late, everything was already wet.

Even though I wasn't very outdoors savvy, I knew I was in trouble, for the guy at the outdoors store had told me that wet down has absolutely no insulating power.

I did have enough sense to pull my dry clothes from my pack and change before I got chilled, putting on a fleece hoodie under my rain jacket and rain pants. I was now warm and dry, but my sleeping bag wasn't going to be much use unless the sun came out soon, which didn't look likely.

A feeling of desolation and hopelessness set in. I was still in shock from dreaming I was being strangled—it had seemed so real. I felt disoriented and afraid.

I sat for some time in the wet forest, on edge, trying to figure out what to do. I finally decided I should leave, though doing so felt like failure to me—I knew I'd come unprepared. I should be carrying a tent for inclement weather like this, or at the very least a waterproof cover fitted to my hammock.

A better outdoorsman could have probably made it all work, but I had no idea how to set up the tarp so it would keep me dry while in a hammock.

I managed to stuff everything into my pack, then turned and headed back down the trail, feeling the entire time like I was being watched and even possibly followed. I recalled the dark creature I'd seen behind me on the trail the previous day, and as time wore on, it felt like it was back. It was truly the creepiest feeling I've ever experienced.

It also seemed really strange that such bad weather had come in so quickly in spite of what the ranger had said about the forecast. It just didn't make sense.

But I hadn't walked more than a half mile when the sun broke through, and I was once again under blue skies. I turned and looked back from where I'd come, and I could see a blackish-blue fog covering everything, a thick bank enveloping the distance, so strange and so abrupt. The sky in all other directions was clear.

I now felt fairly normal, the creepy feeling almost gone, though I was still on edge. Yet it still somehow felt like my very survival was being challenged, and I knew I had to get out of there as quickly as possible. I wondered again about the family whose kids I'd heard, and I hoped they were okay.

I hitched my pack up onto my back and around my hips, getting it settled, when I felt a strange constriction around my neck, as if I were getting a bad sore throat. I instinctively touched it and was surprised to find that it felt very sensitive, as if bruised.

The dream flashed back, and I now wondered if it had indeed actually happened. A strange sense of terror flowed over me, something I'd never felt in my life, making me want to run recklessly down the trail.

I turned back one last time to look at the fog bank, only to find with horror that it was quickly coming my way, slithering along like a huge dark snake.

I turned back to the trail and ran as fast and as hard as I could, pack bouncing against my back, even though I'd snugged it down tightly.

It's difficult to run with a large pack, and my instincts said to ditch it so I could go faster, but my sense of survival said I might need its contents, as I was several long miles from the trailhead, a distance that had taken me two days to hike.

Of course, I was taking my time back then, but there was no way I could return all that much quicker. And even though I was now running, I wasn't in shape to run far—in fact, I was already getting a stitch in my side.

I had to slow down to a fast walk, and I made the mistake of looking behind me, only to see the fog bank even closer. My running had been for naught.

I tried to find a pace that would allow me to move along quickly without getting winded, but I was just too out of shape. I was now panting. I had to stop and take a break, though it was the last thing I wanted to do.

As I stood on the trail, bent over, sides heaving, the fog caught up with me. I could see its dark tendrils creeping around my ankles and feet, and it felt cold and sticky. The panicky feeling of being watched also returned. I could also now smell a strange sickly-sweet odor, kind of like sulphur and pine pitch mixed together. But worst of all, I could hear the children laughing in the distance, laughter that soon faded into a deep whispering that seemed to filter through the trees and shrubs and into my very being.

I again took off running, but the fog was moving too fast, and there was no way I could outrun it. I was soon totally enveloped to the point that I could barely make out the trail.

I knew it was critical that I stay oriented, but it was getting darker and darker by the moment, and I almost felt like I was being overtaken by night.

As I reached to pull out my headlamp, I caught my toe on a tree root in the trail and went down hard, landing on my right knee. The pain was excruciating, and as I lay underneath my heavy pack, my quiet life flashed before me, my life working in a cubicle in the city, and I wanted nothing more than to be back there.

My grand plan to create a new life was crashing down all around me, and even worse, I somehow feared this Yellowstone adventure could be my first and last.

Nothing made sense anymore. Why had I heard children laughing during the night? How could the sound turn into a whispering? What had been behind me when I was on the bear trail? Whatever it was, it was scary enough to frighten bison. Who had tried to strangle me? And why did this fog seem so malevolent?

I had to be losing my mind. I'd spent so much time in the city, being indolent and lazy, that my poor brain couldn't process things going on in the natural world.

I slipped my pack off and managed to pull myself up, using a nearby small tree for leverage. Gingerly putting weight on my knee, it seemed like it would hold me, even though it was sore. I decided that I'd probably cracked or bruised the kneecap. I had to continue on.

I figured I'd probably come a mile at that point, maybe even further. I had no idea how far it was back to my car, but I estimated at least another two or three miles.

I hoisted my pack back on and found that I was able to walk, though slowly, and I had to be very careful. If there was something after me, it looked like I didn't stand a chance.

It was then that I remembered the bear spray. I pulled both cans from my pack and stuck them in the pockets of my rain jacket. I would at least go down fighting.

As I hobbled along, I knew I had no choice but to keep going, no matter what. Even if things hadn't been so weird, there was no way I could spend the night in the damp and cold without a warm sleeping bag. I had no choice but to get back to my car, even if it was after dark. And, in all honesty, there was no way I wanted to spend another night out there.

I stopped and got a water bottle and some gorp and several ibuprofen from my pack. I would continue on as best I could, and maybe these things would help.

The fog was thick, and I had to watch carefully so I didn't trip again or even lose the trail completely. It couldn't be any later than about noon, but it was so dark I could barely make my way. But fortunately, the pain in my knee seem to be abating somewhat, the ibuprofen helping.

I don't know how long I continued, lost in the pain and fog, but it seemed like hours. I stumbled along, barely able to make out the trail, my mind lost in thoughts of my past life and pondering how I got where I was.

For some strange reason, I flashed on a memory, something I hadn't thought about for a long time. I recalled standing and looking out the window of my little rented house, watching as a police car pulled up next door.

My neighbor was kind of a straggly burned-out fellow who spent a lot of time working on his old car. He was outside, looking under the hood, and didn't see the two policemen drive up. They startled him, and as he jumped, they grabbed him, frisked him, then put handcuffs on him and took him away.

I never did find out what he was wanted for, but I never saw him again. After a few weeks, someone came and cleaned out his house, taking all his stuff away, and eventually someone else moved in.

Why I remembered this while out on the trail I don't know, but for some reason I began to feel like it would've been better had they come and taken *me* away instead. I would be better off in jail than out here losing my mind. For some reason, that's how afraid I was, that I would prefer to be in jail than stumbling down that trail in Yellowstone.

I was fatigued, and I couldn't even make out the forest I was walking through, the fog was so thick. I could only assume I was going the right way, as the trail seemed to be gradually going down-hill. I still had no idea how far it was to my car.

I'd lost all track of time—in fact, I felt as if I had no sense of time at all—everything was timeless, time no longer existed. I had to be sleepwalking, yet I knew I was awake because my knee was killing me, and my neck was so sore I could barely turn my head.

To make things even worse, every so often I could hear the whispers come and surround me, just like in my dream. For some reason, I knew I couldn't let on that I was afraid, and after awhile, I even started yelling at them and telling them to go away. I truly felt that I had lost my mind.

After what seemed like forever, I wondered if I were maybe in a dream, a dream where I would be on this long treacherous walk forever, unable to stop, walking on and on.

Just when I thought things couldn't get any worse, well, that's when I heard it. I could hear a scuffling noise coming up behind me, and I wondered if it weren't the bison again. But for some reason I knew it wasn't, perhaps because of the feeling which had returned, an almost supernatural terror of the unknown.

I desperately wanted to run as I heard the heavy footsteps getting closer behind me, but it was all I could do to stumble along. Finally, when whatever it was sounded as if it were right behind me, I decided to turn and face it.

If I were going to die, I would at least die knowing what had killed me, though I somehow knew it wasn't a bear. And when I turned to face it, I immediately wished I hadn't.

What I saw was like nothing I could ever begin to describe, a crea-ture so horrible and terrifying that even trying to remember it makes me want to blank out. At the time, I had no idea what it was, though now I think I do.

It was the legendary Bigfoot, but not like anything I'd ever read about, not like the Bigfoot that disappears into the woods after you see it, or comes into your camp and makes a lot of noise.

It was something much more elemental—more like the true essence of Bigfoot, a creature that goes beyond all mythology and that has evolved through time, becoming more and better adapted to an environment that is as wild as the beast itself—the primal and fiery landscape of Yellowstone.

It had nothing benign about it, and the moment I saw it, I knew its intentions were to kill me. I flashed back to feeling the huge hands around my neck, and I knew now it wasn't a dream. What I didn't know was why it hadn't killed me, why it had stopped, for it could have easily snapped my neck with one movement. I'll never know, but it seemed to have something to do with the whispers.

Instantly, I felt like I was dealing with the supernatural, and I felt as if I were suspended in time and space, that I had shifted from my own reality into another.

But when the giant creature lunged at me, I brought both cans of bear spray up at the same time, hitting the triggers, and a dense fog of capsaicin enveloped it. I knew bear spray would have no effect on something supernatural, and yet the Bigfoot immediately grabbed for its eyes and lurched backwards.

It screamed a sound like nothing I'd ever heard before, a sound that still wakes me in the middle of the night in sheer terror.

There was nothing I could do. I couldn't run, but now I could again hear the whispers all around me, louder and more intense, as the creature fell back in pain. And now, the whispers seemed protective, like they were surrounding me in order to help me.

I turned and hobbled on as best I could down the trail, expecting to be grabbed from behind at any instant. I'd read about the horrors of dying from a bear, and I wondered if death by Bigfoot would be as gruesome. Would anyone ever find my body? Would I become just another missing person statistic?

I could now hear the whispers fading into the distance like a flock of birds, and for some reason, the fog seemed to drift away back behind me. I was soon walking in broad daylight again, though it looked to be late afternoon, as the shadows were lengthening.

After awhile, I stopped to eat a few handfuls of gorp and drink some water, as I could feel my energy seriously lagging. The fog was now a distant dark line far away in the trees.

I thought again of the bear spray, which had obviously worked, which meant that the Bigfoot was real—and this also meant that once it recovered, it would be even angrier, wanting even more to come after me. And this time, with no bear spray to fend it off, I would be doomed.

I had to get to my car, and soon. I felt very disoriented and didn't recognize anything along the trail, and had no idea how far away the trailhead was. I wasn't even sure I was on the right trail anymore.

I have since learned to stop and look back when I'm hiking so things look familiar when I'm returning, but at that time it was just another of my rookie mistakes to not orient myself better.

I stumbled on for another half hour or so when I saw something on the trail ahead of me. I panicked for a moment, then realized I was looking at fellow humans. The emotions I felt were indescribable.

It was a ranger and two young men, and when they saw I was injured, they offered to help me back to my car. They'd been out searching for a couple who'd gone missing several days earlier.

Fortunately, my car was less than a half mile away, and with one of the guys carrying my pack, we made good time, getting back just as it was getting dark.

I was never so happy to see my car! But there was one minor problem, which was that I couldn't drive with my knee messed up, so one of the guys drove me back to the nearest campground, where the others met us and helped set up camp.

I thanked them profusely, and after we made some small talk, the ranger asked if anything odd had happened while I was out backpacking. I told him about the fog and the whispers, but I decided not to mention the Bigfoot lest they all think I was truly crazy. The ranger said something about the Yellowstone Whispers being quite famous, though he'd never heard them himself. He hesitated, as if he wanted to say more, but they all finally left, as it was late.

After making dinner, I climbed into my hammock, happy to be surrounded by people, and tried to go to sleep. I kept opening my eyes and looking at all the people around me in tents, RVs, and pickup campers, and I felt very happy that I was there, safe and secure.

But I had hoped too soon for peace and quiet. I awoke sometime in the middle of the night again in terror, once again feeling those big hands around my neck. I managed to twist around in my hammock and fall to the ground, which woke me.

I wasn't hurt, but I did know that this time it was a dream, and I grabbed my sleeping bag and spent the rest of the night sleeping on the backseat of my car, doors securely locked. It would be the last time I ever slept in a hammock.

The next day, I was still in a lot of pain, but I was now able to drive, so I decided to go up north to the town of Livingston and see a doctor. I went into the urgent care clinic, where they told me I had indeed cracked my kneecap, but there was little they could do for me except give me a prescription for painkillers and advise me to stay off it.

The doctor noticed the red marks around my neck and examined them with concern, asking what had happened. I just made up a bogus story about getting into a fight in a bar, and he let it go at that, telling me to put Neosporin on the places where the skin had been abraded.

Afterwards, I checked into a comfy motel there for a few days, resting and mulling over everything that had happened. Every night, I would dream that I was being choked and would wake up in a dry sweat. And when evening came, I had to fight the urge to flee, to hit the road and go back to the city, any city.

There was something about nightfall that made me restless and unsettled. But the worst was when I would wake in the night hearing the scream of the creature.

One evening, as I was hobbling back and forth in the room,

forcing myself to not run away, it dawned on me just how close I still was to Yellowstone.

Livingston is only about an hour from the north gate, and even though I'd backpacked more in the southern end of the park, all that wilderness was a simple hour away. Actually, it was even closer, for Livingston is surrounded by mountains that are home to grizzlies and wolves—and most likely Bigfoot. The wilderness was almost right out my door.

I now felt like I was having a mental breakdown. I had to get a grip on myself. What about my plans to see all the national parks? Wilderness was part of the definition of a national park, and if I couldn't deal with the wilds, I might as well go back to the city, get another job, and go ahead and gradually die from inactivity and boredom.

Was that what I wanted? In a way, I felt like I was suffering from PTSD. Maybe I needed to see a therapist. But who would believe such a story? I would probably end up being committed.

But I had to talk to someone. I recalled the look the ranger had given me as he left after we had discussed the fog and the Yellowstone Whispers. I had the distinct feeling that he knew I'd left something out.

Maybe I should go back down to the park and talk to him, but the thought of going back into Yellowstone gave me the shivers. What if my car broke down and no one came around to help me out in the middle of nowhere?

I thought about it long and hard, then realized that with the millions of visitors there every year, my fears of no one to help were irrational. I would go back the next day.

It took awhile to track the ranger down, but I finally found him in the same campground where I'd fallen from my hammock. He seemed surprised to see me, and asked if I'd checked back in with the Visitor Center to let them know I'd come out.

I told him that I hadn't realized I was supposed to, and he said he would call and and let them know. The last thing they wanted was another search in the park.

He invited me to sit down at a picnic table with him and share a cold soda. He then got to talking about the missing couple, who they still hadn't found. Had I seen or heard anything unusual? The last place they'd been seen was on the same trail I'd come down.

I once again got the feeling he wanted to ask me something, yet was hesitant to do so. I told him I hadn't heard or seen any other people.

I recalled the children's laughter in the night. Would that have anything to do with the missing couple? Should I tell him about it?

The ranger then asked me how my knee was doing, and I told him it was cracked. He asked how I'd managed to fall hard enough to crack my kneecap, and I told him I'd been running. He looked at me really funny, and asked if I'd been running from something or somebody, maybe the same somebody who had left the black bruises around my neck.

It was then that I knew he was aware of strange happenings, and I decided to tell him everything. After all, I'd come down expressly to talk to him, and I needed to clear the air and see what he might know.

It took some time for me to get it all out, as it sounded so outlandish, but I could tell from the look on his face that he believed me. When I was finished, he simply looked at me and said, "Do you realize how lucky you are?"

I replied, "Lucky? My first backpacking trip ever and something tries to kill me? I don't think I could've picked a worse place, nor been so unlucky."

The ranger replied, "Nobody understands the whispers, though many have heard them. It's one of the great mysteries of the park. They were first reported by early explorers, mostly in the vicinity of Yellowstone and Shoshone lakes. But even fewer have seen what we call the Yellowstone Fog. The fog isn't something you want to see, for those who have seen it have typically had encounters with a very malevolent creature. Nobody knows what causes the fog, but some think it's related to the same intricate underground system that causes the geysers and hot springs."

He continued, "None of the rangers will discuss this in public. There's no reasoning behind it, though some think the creature lives where the fog is prevalent and uses it as a cover. How the whispers are involved is a true mystery."

"But back to being lucky. This is not anything I want you to repeat, but we have found a number of missing people in areas where the fog has also been seen, and several have been dead from broken necks. That's what I mean when I say you don't realize how lucky you are. The ones who have survived have told the same story you just told me. I'm worried to death that we'll find that missing couple the same way."

I asked, "Do you think the creature heard the couple and left me right as it was getting ready to kill me?"

"Anything's possible. It would explain it, but who knows why the creature didn't kill you. It may have had something to do with the whispers. But I will tell you that a number of rangers have seen Bigfoot, and one nicknamed Action Jackson has even written in print about his encounters—he was a highly respected ranger in his day."

We talked for a long time, and it was dark when I drove on back through the park and back to Livingston. I was surprised at my courage to drive in the dark through the park, but it really wasn't too bad.

I was anxious to get back to my room and away from the wilds, even though I saw a beautiful Great Horned Owl in my headlights on the way back. I also got to again see the Milky Way through my windshield, as I was too scared to get out to really look at it. Even through glass, it was the most incredible sight I've ever seen—well, almost anyway. I think the creature will always hold that dubious honor.

It's very unlikely that I'll ever backpack again, but I will go hiking, though not alone. I've been back to Yellowstone since then, but mostly just to see the geysers, and I stayed in places with lots of tourists around. Oh, and I learned later that the couple was found, safe and sound, fortunately.

Not long after all this happened, I came to grips with my fears and realized I would never be the same. I would never be able to sleep out under the stars and feel comfortable. So, I bought a small RV and now travel with friends when I can, though I do sometimes go alone.

At the time of this telling, I've seen 22 of the parks, and I'll soon be on my way to Alaska to see the ones there. Talk about wilderness! But I'm traveling with friends, so I'm not going anywhere out there alone. And I now have two wonderful rescue dogs who are my lifetime buddies and who make me feel safe at night.

I learned a lot about nature and myself on that ill-fated backpacking trip, and I have the utmost respect for the natural world and my place in it. I know I'll never be a seasoned outdoorsman, and that's okay, for I've learned my limits and what I feel comfortable with. And I've also learned that there are things out there that we know very little about.

Personally, I'm happy to keep it that way.

ABOUT THE AUTHOR

Rusty Wilson is a fly-fishing guide based in Colorado and Montana. He's well-known for his dutch-oven cookouts and campfires, where he's heard some pretty wild stories about the creatures in the woods, especially Bigfoot.

Whether you're a Bigfoot believer or not, we hope you enjoyed this book, and we know you'll enjoy Rusty's many others, the first of which is *Rusty Wilson's Bigfoot Campfire Stories*, as well as his popular *Bigfoot: The Dark Side*, and *The Creature of Lituya Bay*, as well as *Chasing After Bigfoot: My Search for North America's Most Elusive Creature*.

Rusty's books come in ebook format, as well as in print and audio.

You'll also enjoy the first book in the Bud Shumway mystery series, a Bigfoot mystery, *The Ghost Rock Cafe*.

Other offerings from Yellow Cat Publishing include an RV series by RV expert Sunny Skye, which includes *Living the Simple RV Life*. And don't forget to check out the books by Sunny's friend, Bob Davidson: *On the Road with Joe*, and *Any Road, USA*. And finally, saving the best for last, you'll love Roger Dean Miller's comedy thriller, *Bombing Hoffman*.